"WHO *ARE* YOU, SIR?"

It was on the tip of his tongue to give the answer he had given for most of his seven-and-twenty years, out of long habit. He had only recently learned that he had lived his life under an alias; all his life he had thought his name to be Peter White. This new name sat ill on his tongue.

Miss Hampton stared at him, silently urging him to answer her question.

He offered her a bow. "I am Fane Peter Westby," he said, looking up and finding the start of surprise he had expected to see in her eyes. "I am Lord Galbreth's son."

Miss Hampton gasped aloud, and shook her head, but she surely saw the familial resemblance. Even Fane had seen the likeness in the miniature he had found among his dead mother's things.

"I—!" Miss Hampton sputtered. "Fane Westby is missing . . . has been gone all these years . . . !"

He gazed wordlessly into her eyes, and he saw the moment when her astonishment turned into acceptance of the truth.

WATCH FOR THESE ZEBRA REGENCIES

LADY STEPHANIE   (0-8217-5341-X, $4.50)
by Jeanne Savery
Lady Stephanie Morris has only one true love: the family estate she has managed ever since her mother died. But then Lord Anthony Rider arrives on her estate, claiming he has plans for both the land and the woman. Stephanie soon realizes she's fallen in love with a man whose sensual caresses will plunge her into a world of peril and intrigue . . . a man as dangerous as he is irresistible.

BRIGHTON BEAUTY   (0-8217-5340-1, $4.50)
by Marilyn Clay
Chelsea Grant, pretty and poor, naively takes school friend Alayna Marchmont's place and spends a month in the country. The devastating man had sailed from Honduras to claim his promised bride, Miss Marchmont. An affair of the heart may lead to disaster . . . unless a resourceful Brighton beauty finds a way to stop a masquerade and keep a lord's love.

LORD DIABLO'S DEMISE   (0-8217-5338-X, $4.50)
by Meg-Lynn Roberts
The sinfully handsome Lord Harry Glendower was a gambler and the black sheep of his family. About to be forced into a marriage of convenience, the devilish fellow engineered his own demise, never having dreamed that faking his death would lead him to the heavenly refuge of spirited heiress Gwyn Morgan, the daughter of a physician.

A PERILOUS ATTRACTION   (0-8217-5339-8, $4.50)
by Dawn Aldridge Poore
Alissa Morgan is stunned when a frantic passenger thrusts her baby into Alissa's arms and flees, having heard rumors that a notorious highwayman posed a threat to their coach. Handsome stranger Hugh Sebastian secretly possesses the treasured necklace the highwayman seeks and volunteers to pose as Alissa's husband to save her reputation. With a lost baby and missing necklace in their care, the couple embarks on a journey into peril—and passion.

Available wherever paperbacks are sold, or order direct from the Publisher. Send cover price plus 50¢ per copy for mailing and handling to Penguin USA, P.O. Box 999, c/o Dept. 17109, Bergenfield, NJ 07621. Residents of New York and Tennessee must include sales tax. DO NOT SEND CASH.

THE RELUCTANT LORD

Teresa DesJardien

Zebra Books
Kensington Publishing Corp.

http://www.zebrabooks.com

ZEBRA BOOKS are published by

Kensington Publishing Corp.
850 Third Avenue
New York, NY 10022

First Printing: July, 1997
10 9 8 7 6 5 4 3 2 1

Printed in the United States of America

Dedicated to Barbara Cruz:
Thanks for always believing in me.

One

Fane Westby looked up from the dust of the road beneath his bootheels to see the gatehouse for which he searched, and sighed heavily. Even to his own ears the sound was a curious mixture of relief and aversion. Having walked at least two miles to arrive here, he'd had time to begin to wonder if he'd somehow missed the estate. However, the large and ornate ironwork bars of the gates had been described to him, so even though Fane had never set eyes on them before, he knew he had found his destination.

Now that he had arrived, he almost wished he had another two miles to go, or ten, or a score. But he doubted that he would come to any manner of conclusion as to his future even with the time it would take to walk a hundred miles. His future's direction lay within those unbending gates, within the grand house he knew must be set back so it would not be seen from the public road. It was only by venturing within that Fane could determine how he would lead the rest of his life.

The hackney he had hired to carry him from the heart of London had refused to leave its route to take him beyond the posting inn in the rural village of Kendall Town. The inn had failed to produce any local farmer or squire who might offer him a seat on their equipage, so Fane had hoisted his two heavy valises and set off on foot.

The walk through a June-warmed countryside had shown him a vista that was even more foreign to his eyes than London itself had been. The hillsides were green and rolling, their trees running in neat rows that divided the fields, not thick and wild and untamed as were the forests just ten miles outside his home in Philadelphia. None of which should surprise him, he thought in sour amusement, for everything about this journey had been odd or unsettlingly new. Indeed, the purpose of the journey itself was the oddest thing of all.

Besides, there was a reason he ought never have set foot in England, a reason that only Fane knew—Fane and one other man: an Englishman who did no credit to his country. While there was no reason to think the two might meet, not here in the rural countryside, far outside the licentious offerings there were surely to be had more easily and readily in London—it was equally true that Fane had no idea where the scoundrel lived. Should they happen to meet face to face here on this country lane, it would take but a few words to the local constabulary, and Fane had no doubt he would find himself in shackles.

There was nothing for it, however. Fane had come, and the threat of his presence, his pseudonym, being found out was a small thing next to his need to close a circle that had begun twenty-four years ago.

It only added insult to injury when he spied the mechanism that locked the twin gates shut from the inside, as if specially there to bar him from the meeting he sought. It was clear from the tall weeds growing before the gatehouse door that no gatekeeper waited within to attend the gate.

Fane hung his head for a moment, and issued a weary sigh when his glance took in the ruined shine of his boots. It was utterly in keeping with the strangeness of the day, of the awkward meeting that would occur—should he ever gain entrance to the property—that he was forced to arrive dusty and disheveled. He would have far preferred to appear at his best before the estate's master, Lord Galbreth.

"Perhaps I'll first be given the chance to put myself to rights," Fane said aloud.

"You are to move on, sir," came a voice, causing Fane to jerk his head up and stare into the handsome face of a young woman seated on a horse just the other side of the locked gate.

"I never heard your approach," he said, rather stupidly he supposed.

"I have been waiting here awhile, watching you," the young woman said in a clear and commanding voice that belied the youth of her features. "If you were thinking of climbing the gate and trespassing, you must think again."

She made no motion on her own account, but her horse sidled to the left, and Fane saw then through the sturdy iron bars of the gate that the young woman held a pistol. The barrel rested parallel to her leg where it crossed on her sidesaddle under a deep blue riding habit—a relaxed posture that still managed to suggest competence. In fact, everything about the woman's posture suggested confidence and capability, despite the fact that she incongruously wore a much-stained apron pinned atop her habit. Odd, that.

Too, there were flowers gaily fixed among the weaving of the long earth-brown plait that was tossed forward over her left shoulder, as well as in her grey mount's plaited mane. The dark brown eyes with which she gazed at him made him think she could be a gypsy, were it not for the glowing white skin only lightly pinked by the sun's touch. And like a gypsy, she held the pistol with unmistakable assurance and warning. Fane found himself relieved that the pistol was not pointed at his chest.

"Well?" she questioned, one brow arching as her lips thinned with admonition. "Are you going to stand there all day?"

"No," he told her. "I am going to enter that gate."

"I think not."

Fane deliberately allowed his valises to drop into the dust of the road, even as he examined her face and figure for some indication of who she might be. He came to no conclusion, and was in fact puzzled to see that behind her saddle hung two leather bags filled to overflowing with wildflowers and weeds. That at least explained the stained apron. Was she the local midwife, perhaps, or an herbalist who quacked the locals with a series of potions and salves? Or perhaps a kitchen maid sent to harvest the land's bounty? But what manner of kitchen maid rode about with a pistol at the ready?

"Do you work about this estate?" he asked doubtfully, for surely neither wisewomen nor servants owned riding habits here any more than they did in America.

"No," she said at once, and then added, "Well, not strictly speaking."

Her speech was cultured, he noted. "Are you a member of the family?"

"No. But enough talk. I will give you one minute to pick up your bags and—"

"Then I wonder that you suggest I might desire to trespass," he interrupted. "For it would seem you do so yourself, being neither employed here nor part of the family."

"I am not trespassing!" she said, her tone rising a little in agitation. "I have been given permission to pass over these grounds. I very much doubt you can say the same."

"Strictly speaking," he echoed her choice of words, "I suppose you are correct."

She did not narrow her gaze, but all the same it was clear she was growing out of all patience with him. Tired and travel-weary as he was, he knew a moment's regret that he had caused the young lady to take him in disfavor. Surely there would be enough new faces to take him in disfavor in the days to come.

"Why do you carry a pistol?" he asked, eyeing the weapon.

"To shoot people with."

He lifted his eyebrows in surprise. "You do this often?"

"Only when aggravated beyond all bearing," she said, and he did not hear any mark of amusement in her tone. "I assure you, sir, I am quite capable of firing it, and of hitting my target."

He nodded his acceptance of the statement, think-ing of the half-dozen American women he could name who knew how to prime and fire a weapon, and all of them city-dwellers, not country lasses. It might not be a feminine art, but it certainly was a skill the ladies could acquire.

"You need not feel you must demonstrate your abilities, I pray, at least as regards myself." He glanced at the bags of wildflowers hanging from either side of the horse. "But perhaps it is just as well you are armed, for you never know when you will have to fend off a particularly vicious bee."

She pursed her lips in disdain. "I am glad you are capable of amusing yourself, sir, but I believe the lord of this land would wish me to demand that you move along. At once," she stated firmly, one hand steady on the reins, the other just as steady on the pistol.

For a moment Fane did not speak, wondering what this woman's connection to Lord Galbreth could be. Not that it mattered. To see Galbreth was his sole reason for coming to England. Depending on the reception Fane received, he might not stay long enough to ever meet this curious female again.

"Move along, you say," Fane said, losing interest in sparring with the woman. No slip of a girl would delay him a minute longer. Although that was not correct: this woman was not a "slip of a girl." She was clearly young—twenty perhaps—but of a medium or better height, and possessed of a way of holding herself that many a matron would envy as a model of graceful authority. "Is it not possible I have business here? Do I look to you like a ruffian or a thief who must be turned away, if the house is to retain its silver?"

She considered him for a long moment, but instead of answering his questions, she posed one of her own.

"Are you perchance an American, sir?" She made the word "American" sound as fantastic as she might the word "Hottentot."

It had been his intention to hide and suppress his prejudice against the English as a race, to reserve judgment, especially now that he stood on their soil. However, in two minutes' conversation, this girl had managed to bring his antipathy instantly to the surface.

"Such a direct question! You surprise me. And this after having spent weeks on board ship being told how infallibly polite the English are," he said, hearing the sneer in his own voice.

"On board ship?" she echoed, pulling her reins more tightly in, to keep her restless mount from tossing its head.

"I came from America. Just to call upon Lord Galbreth."

She appeared skeptical and poised to demand further proof, so without waiting for her words, he provided it by lifting his left hand. There, on his pinkie finger, sat a broad gold signet ring, an ornate letter "G" decorating its surface.

"Do you know this ring?" he asked, but he needn't have, for he could tell by her startled expression that she did. He had found it among his mother's belongings. It seemed he had been correct to bring it, that it might act as a key to open doors long since locked behind him.

"I recognize the signet," she said, her eyes wide. "I . . . ! I beg your pardon. It seems clear you have some matter of business here, for Lord Galbreth to have sent you his ring."

He did not correct her misassumption.

"Do forgive my caution, but Lord Galbreth has so few visitors anymore, now his health is so poor—"

"His health is poor?" he interrupted her abruptly.

"Indeed, sir."

"How poor?"

She stared down at him, some of the original haughtiness returning. "How is that you do not know?"

"I did not wait upon his return letter."

She pursed her lips, seeming to accept for the moment his imperfect explanation. "The truth is, sir, the doctors question his chances at recovery."

Fane stared in return, then glanced down the long drive that obviously led to the house, its presence hidden by the curve of the lane and the tall trees lining it. Lord Galbreth waited within . . . and in failing health.

"I am sorry if I have alarmed you with this news," said the woman. "But with Lord Galbreth so ill, it has fallen to those of us about the estate to challenge the right of callers to be here. You might be surprised to learn what manner of ruffian or cad come wandering about an estate when the master lies ill and abed."

Fane glanced at the deserted gatehouse and its obvious neglect. "Not so surprised, I think. But I guess I must thank you for finding me to be something other than a ruffian or a cad."

"I am afraid it is only the ring that convinces me of your proper intentions," she said dryly, and then to his surprise, she offered him a smile.

The smile softened her look, making the most of features that were not traditionally soft and feminine. She was not wildly pretty, even if she might aspire to the title were she one to use clever artifice, but there was a quality to her features that Fane's mama had sometimes called "handsome" as regarded a certain feminine appearance. Her smile, on the other hand, was rather dazzling, changing her expression from stern to receptive, and this from only a mild turning up of her lips. Fane stared for a moment, then shook his head once, as though to clear it of clouds.

He parted his lips to protest that there must surely be more to his own personal appearance that would cause a lady to trust him than merely the ring, but she was already urging her horse forward, positioning it next to the twin gates. She reached for the latching mechanism that locked the gate from within, turned her mount's head, and retreated enough for Fane to be able to swing open one side of the two gates.

He lifted his bags and carried them onto the estate, setting them once again in the dust after kicking the gate behind him.

He crossed his arms and set his feet in a wide and solid stance—an undeniable mark of those who had lived in America, as if they had all the room in the world in which to stretch out their legs, as he had been told by many an Englishman aboard the ship.

"Tell me, Miss—?"

"Hampton," she supplied.

"Miss Hampton, please tell me how it is that you find yourself serving as guardian to these grounds."

She considered him for a moment, and he noticed she still had the pistol in hand, and that she kept her horse away from his reach, presumably to avoid allowing him the chance to seize the bridle. Clever girl, not to wholly trust a stranger, ring or no.

"All of Lord Galbreth's neighbors have served so when called upon by chance, since Lord Galbreth's health began to fail," she explained. "I have seen for myself that once a certain element learn that the master is no longer in full command, they begin to circle, to see what pickings might be had. I have been happy to chase away the poachers and rabble such as it has been my misfortune to discover."

"That is brave of you," Fane said, even as he belatedly realized the pretty young lady rode unaccompanied by an attendant. The lack might have surprised him less in the rural districts of America, but he knew comely young Englishwomen did not often have such freedom, not even in the countryside. The "miss" in her name assured him there was no husband to forbid her riding about alone, so it might be guessed she had a tolerant parent, one apparently unconcerned with seeing to her safekeeping. Too, it was possible Miss Hampton was just a headstrong young lady who did as she pleased . . . given the pistol, the lack of a bonnet, and her peculiar garb, this seemed as likely a possibility as any other.

Though, perhaps the countryside of England was a less wild and unpredictable place than that of America could be. Despite all his mother's talk of her beloved England, there was so much he did not know about this land.

"You have trouble with poachers and rabble, you say?" He frowned.

"Yes, and the situation is only likely to become worse long before it improves. I understand the likely heir is engaged in the fighting in Russia, and so may be months learning of his inheritance."

"The heir?" Fane echoed. Galbreth must be ill indeed if there was such ready talk of an heir.

"A distant nephew, as I understand it."

"Lord Galbreth's heir?"

She nodded, frowning at him. "Of whom else would we be speaking? That is his signet you wear."

He ignored her question. "Just how ill is Lord Galbreth?"

"He has pneumonia. But there is hope." She lowered her lashes for a moment, and added, "Some hope."

"I am relieved to learn I am not too late," he said, meaning every word.

It surprised him how news of Galbreth's illness rolled around sickly in his stomach. Thank God he had left America when he had.

He shook off the unpleasant sensation, turning his attention back to the young woman. "It is good of you to see the property is protected. But you must desist in future, Miss Hampton. I would not wish you to be harmed. If you learn of any disturbance, you must ride to the house, and inform me of the matter."

"You, sir?" She fixed a level eye on him. "Are you a new secretary? Or Lord Galbreth's new steward perhaps?"

He shook his head, but before he could reply she rapped out another question. "Who *are* you, sir?"

It was on the tip of his tongue to give the answer he had given for most of his seven-and-twenty years, out of long habit. He had only recently learned that he had lived his life under an alias; all his life he had thought his name to be Peter White. Peter Fane White. This new name sat ill on his tongue.

Miss Hampton stared at him, silently urging him to answer her question.

He offered her a bow. "I am Fane Peter Westby," he said, looking up and finding the start of surprise he had expected to see in her eyes. "I am Lord Galbreth's son."

Miss Hampton gasped aloud, and shook her head, but she surely saw the familial resemblance. Even Fane had seen the likeness in the miniature he had found among his dead mother's things.

"I—!" Miss Hampton sputtered. "Fane Westby is missing . . . has been gone all these years . . . !"

He gazed wordlessly into her eyes, and he saw the moment when her astonishment turned into acceptance of the truth.

Her hands must have gone lax on the reins, for her horse stepped forward, lowering its head for an attempt at nibbling the nearby tall grass. Miss Hampton visibly gathered her wits along with the horse's reins, pulling up its head as she offered Fane a curt nod. "Please excuse me," she murmured, and before he could respond, had turned her horse, nudged it in the side, and set the beast to trotting away.

Fane stared after the retreating rider. He had expected surprise, even shock, but he could not guess what it was about this name he bore that had caused the lady to abruptly depart in such a distracted air.

What an odd moment—and a curious young lady.

Grimly he turned to glance down the long drive that led to the house, and turned his thoughts to what lay ahead there. His father lived in that house, the father he had never known, a father who was reportedly very ill.

Part of him was leery of coming face-to-face with the man who had impelled his mother into the desperate act of fleeing England . . . but there was another part of him, a part uncomfortably traitorous to his mother's memory, that wished to meet the man who had sired him, to measure the man's worth for himself, for there had been a handful of times when Fane had, in all truth, had to question his mother's judgment.

It was too late to change his mind, he thought to himself with a small mirthless laugh. He was here, and he must go forward. He wondered if this moment would have felt less odd if he had not had that curious encounter with Miss Hampton? There was no knowing the answer to that.

Fane sighed heavily, and picked up his valises. He began the last leg of the walk toward Westby Hall, keenly aware that at long last he had arrived at the strange intersection where his past would meet his future.

Two

"Aunt Silvia!" Marietta Hampton cried, half out of breath in agitation as she slid from her sidesaddle to the ground. "Aunt Silvia!" she called again as she secured her gelding's reins to the fence.

She spotted her aunt as she came to the open door of the small home the two shared. Silvia was drying her stained hands on a towel, obviously having just been interrupted in the middle of dyeing a new batch of wool.

"Marietta," she called in return, "do come and tell me what you think of this shade of blue."

Marietta shook her head in mild agitation that her aunt had failed to sense the urgency behind her call. Her eccentric aunt was certainly an intelligent woman, but given over to her own thoughts, and little affected by the rhythm and gossip of village life as it revolved around their home. Silvia had never expended much energy on fretting, and since Marietta had come to live here three months ago, had happily left all the worrying to her more worldly niece. But this news was too worrisome for Marietta to bear alone; she made a point of taking the few steps down the path, that she might gather up her aunt's hands, to fully capture that lady's attention.

"I have news. Important news," Marietta said on a breathless sigh. "I do not know how this will affect us, but I cannot think it must be good."

At Aunt Silvia's steady and mildly surprised stare, Marietta went on. "I just met a man who claims to be Fane Westby!"

Silvia's eyes widened. "Aaron's son?" she asked. "Aaron's son has truly come?"

"Why, Aunt Silvia! You are not the slightest bit surprised. You knew he had been found?" Marietta said, her shock ringing in her words.

Silvia nodded. "Aaron told me the boy had written—all of a sudden, just like that! Although I suppose he is hardly a boy now, as it must be close to five-and-twenty years since he disappeared."

"Why did you not tell me?" Marietta cried.

Silvia covered one of her niece's hands with both of her own, patting gently. "I thought such news must upset you, my dear—you must admit it has done just that! And Aaron had nothing but this man's claims to tell him if this was truly his son or not, so there's no saying where the truth lies. And who was to say if the man would truly come to England as he wrote he would? It all seemed best to let it lie, until there was more word. Oh dear, I can see you are not pleased with me."

"Oh, Aunt Silvia, can you not see how this might change everything? How I wish you had long since insisted that Lord Galbreth—"

"Tut, tut! You know I will not insist on anything. Besides, Aaron is going to get well, and everything shall go on as it has before, you will see. But, my dear, do tell me what this Fane Westby looks like."

Marietta blew out an exasperated breath, but there was no point in berating her aunt. Silvia was deliberately unwilling to consider the possibility that her lover, Aaron, Lord Galbreth, might be too ill to recover, that this stranger, this unknown factor, might inherit the estate upon which the two ladies resided.

"I should think he would be tall, as Aaron is such a tall man," Aunt Silvia pressed.

Marietta gave a resigned sigh. "He is a large man. Tall, yes, and broad-shouldered, with brown hair and blue eyes. In truth, he looks the very picture of your Aaron. And he had a ring, with the ornate 'G' just like the ones on the gates."

"Oh, that *does* bode well! How very nice for Aaron. How remarkable!" Aunt Silvia murmured happily. She bobbed her head, looked to the ground, and then back up at her taller niece, something suspiciously close to tears teetering on her lashes as a tremulous smile threatened her lips. "If this is true, if the man is his son, you can but imagine how pleased Aaron must be."

Marietta nodded, saying nothing as she tried to imagine the reaction this news of a son's return would bring from Aaron Westby, the fourth Baron Galbreth.

Marietta was the only person, besides his valet, who knew that Lord Galbreth and Aunt Silvia had been lovers these fifteen years past. While Marietta could not say she approved of the unsanctified liaison, she was in no position to look down her nose at the only relative who could be counted on to give her a home following the revelation of Marietta's own disgrace. Three months ago she might have wished to believe that affairs of the heart could be ordered all neat and tidy and tied with a fancy bow, but now she knew far better.

"This man, the one claiming to be Mr. Westby—he has come from America," Marietta said as she moved back to her horse and untied the reins from the fence.

"Indeed! Aaron did not say. I had assumed the fellow wrote from Australia." Aunt Silvia walked at her side as they moved toward the small paddock and simple roofed stall that served as the gelding's only shelter. "But America! So that is where Lady Galbreth fled to when she left Aaron! He always thought she must have gone to Australia."

Marietta nodded, having heard the tale of how Lord Galbreth's agent had reported that an unnamed woman and babe had disembarked in that faraway continent two months after the lady's disappearance from her home. Indeed, the rumor was all part of the local conjectures, one of many, that had sprung up after the disappearance of Lord Galbreth's brash young wife some twenty-odd years ago.

"It is no wonder that the trail went cold from that port," Aunt Silvia went on. "Obviously, one way or the other, Lady Galbreth must have settled in America."

"So it would seem," Marietta agreed.

"She is dead, you know. Lady Galbreth. Or at least that is what this fellow claiming to be Fane Westby wrote. Aaron thinks she changed her name, to hide all these years. Mrs. Smith, or Jones, or Johnson. Something of that nature."

Marietta shook her head, as much for Lady Galbreth's machinations and her death, as for her aunt's blithe description of them. Aunt Silvia was clearly unflustered by this turn of events, for she reached to remove the saddlebags from the horse and rest them on the fence, and then to remove the horse's sidesaddle with no greater emotion than a gentle smile. As always, it would be left to Marietta to deal with any consequences brought on by this change in circumstances.

In the three months since her arrival at her aunt's home, Marietta had grown largely accustomed to the lady's unconventional—and rather scatterwitted—ways, and if she was still not quite used to the fact her aunt had chosen for all these years to be a man's mistress (even be it quietly so), it had not stood in the way of Marietta becoming enormously fond of her aunt. After all, they were both rebels, of one sort or another, and to condemn her aunt was to condemn herself. That Marietta could not do, not even after all she had suffered as a result of her decision to choose her own way, to defy her father's will.

Still, sometimes she thought Aunt Silvia had made some poor choices, not least of which was her decision not to marry Lord Galbreth. He could have long since petitioned Parliament to have his wife declared legally dead, but he had never done so, and Aunt Silvia had never requested that he take that step.

Silvia's indifference to marriage was no charade on her aunt's part either, Marietta knew, for it was Aunt Silvia's inability to live conventionally that had caused her to be cut off from the greater family. Marietta's contact with her aunt had been quite limited . . . that is until Marietta was labeled as much a "foolish, evil harridan as her aunt" and shuffled off to live in Kendall Town outside London.

"What are we to do with Marietta?" her father had

roared at Marietta's mother three months ago. "Why, we shall send her to that mad sister of yours who claims to be a 'Free Thinker,' that's what we shall do! And may they have much joy of one another!"

Curiously enough, his words had taken on a prophetic ring of truth, for while there was not much in the way of worldly goods in their household, the two women had found a world of contentment and camaraderie with one another, despite the differences in their ages and dispositions.

Marietta reached to remove the gelding's bridle, also pulling free the flowers she had plaited into its mane. The horse shook its head, and snorted softly before lowering its head to snuffle at the flowers that had fallen to the dirt. Apparently finding them lacking, the gelding then moved off to see if there were anything of interest in his feed trough, rather optimistically, for a chronic lack of funds seldom allowed for a portion of oats.

"Aaron's son has returned," Aunt Silvia repeated on a sigh, shaking her head as though in pleased disbelief.

Marietta spun to face her. "Oh, Aunt Silvia, I am pleased for Lord Galbreth, too, but do you not see? If this man is legitimate, his presence might well change everything for us!"

"That is true. But you assume the worst—"

"What else am I to assume?"

"Aaron's health will improve," Aunt Silvia said with the kind of blind hope that comes from not wanting to look directly at a hard truth.

"But, even if it does, will you speak to him again? Will you please, please ask him to give us a paper, a document, something that shows he has altered his will as he promised he would? Are we to keep this house, or not? It is so very important that we be absolutely sure he has arranged—"

"Tush, now. You know I have no inclination to ask him for anything like that. He has said he will do it, and that is well enough for me," Aunt Silvia said, pulling from the saddlebags her old-fashioned pistol, the one Marietta carried with her when she rode the estate searching for the flora that would provide colors for homemade dyes. Silvia tucked the pistol under her arm, and fussed with the flowers, needlessly rearranging them in the bags. "I never wanted so much as a penny from him. That was not what our love was all about," she stated the oft-repeated sentiment, and Marietta despaired to see the stubborn set of her aunt's chin. "It is too mercenary by far to ask for written assurances."

"It is never that! You have to think about what could happen. Where should we live if we had to leave here?" Marietta insisted. "We scratch out an existence as it stands now! How could we ever pay rent elsewhere?"

Aunt Silvia's only response was to shake her head, silently acknowledging she had no ideas.

Because they paid no rent for using Lord Galbreth's dower house, they just managed to afford the cost of food and fuel and other necessities from the small stipend Aunt Silvia's grandmama had bequeathed to her, and the even smaller one Papa's solicitor forwarded each month for Marietta's keep. At first Marietta had despaired at ever living above the meanest level of poverty. She had felt like the burden she surely was on her aunt, and had spent two days listlessly grieving and wandering her aunt's home as if she could somehow find her old, comfortable life if only she looked hard enough for it.

Early on the third morning with her aunt, the sound of a lamb's bleating in the field outside had made Marietta think of how in autumn it would be time to harvest the creature's wool . . . and it had suddenly struck her that she had the ability to create additional income. She had a talent she could sell: weaving.

Fortunately, her father had sent two important things with her into banishment: her horse and her beloved loom. The horse gave her a way to deliver any goods, and the loom (a gift from her mother, given five years ago to help Marietta idle away a sickly winter) now gave her a way to produce a salable product.

She had ridden into the Kendall Town High Street, shown her small collection of prior works (six shawls she had made over the years for her own pleasure), and amazed herself by convincing the shopkeeper, Mr. Hissop, to sell them for her.

The partial advance payment he had given her for the shawls had cast out any last doubts she might have harbored regarding the lamentable matter of engaging in trade.

Three months of moderate sales later, not to mention a great deal of hard work, had hardly proven enough to allow both ladies to breathe a sigh of relief, but at least they now had cause for hope. Marietta dared think only of putting enough aside to brave the winter, but over time, please God, they just might earn enough extra income to improve their entire lot in life. For now she could turn her gaze away from the tempting sight of beautiful, lace-edged fans propped in the shop windows that called out to her young, feminine heart, and concentrate her thoughts on devising pretty patterned goods for other, richer ladies to buy.

But now, another threat menaced. The simple truth was that if they suddenly found they had to pay rent, there would not be enough money to go on. They could eat less meat, and perhaps more carefully watch how much coal they burned come the winter cold. They could give up the few pennies they paid the local lad Eddie to wash the raw sheep's wool, which would mean that Marietta and her aunt must do it themselves (complete with the necessity of wearing salve and gloves to bed each night, to try and maintain some illusion of ladylike skin). But they must grant Mr. Hissop the six percent of proceeds he demanded to sell their goods through his shop—for the only other choice was to sell from their home, and that Aunt Silvia had refused to do from the very first moment that Marietta had suggested selling the shawls at all.

"It is one thing to be thought an eccentric old woman engaging in trade—" Aunt Silvia had said in her most stubborn tone of voice.

"You speak as though you are an ancient," Marietta had interrupted. "You are not yet fifty!"

"As I was saying, it is one thing to have myself thought of as the county's eccentric, but quite another to have that mark put upon you, my girl!" Aunt Silvia had stated unequivocally. "I will *not* conduct trade from my home."

So, they'd had very few choices. They *must* be able to go on living where they were.

And now, here came Mr. Westby, claiming to be the

son and heir. The dower house was not entailed, was not part of the property that must be inherited by the heir—but what reason would this stranger have to allow them to remain, free of rent, all the same? There was no reason to suppose Lord Galbreth's son would be kindly disposed toward his father's *amour.* Oh, if only Marietta knew for a certainty that the house was legally, bindingly granted to her aunt, that the son would have no right to cast them out should he come to inherit the estate!

Although, she allowed herself to acknowledge, what guarantee was such a document anyway? What if the father changed the will to grant everything, utterly unfettered, to the son? What if the son convinced the father to change the will to the same purpose? Today's document could be tomorrow's fish wrap!

"Are you in pain, Marietta? I have never heard you make a moaning sound like that before," Aunt Silvia asked in concern.

"I am as right as I can be," Marietta said, and did not deign to expand on the statement. Instead she moved to hoist the heavy saddlebags. There was no servant to order to carry them for her, and no maid to do the messy work of crushing or drying the flowers they held. No one to do her bidding . . . proof, if she needed it, that she had come down in life.

Still, she could not wholly regret the path she had chosen. What she did regret was that it had involved hurting someone else, even if the horrid Mr. Sharr had been all that was deserving of an injury. There was no point in wasting time on regrets, anyway, even if she could not quite soothe the sting of resentments she yet harbored—and the biggest resentment of all was knowing she had very little control over what would happen next in her life.

The two women went into the house, her aunt moving through to the fenced back garden to tend to her steamy, smelly dyeing of the most recently spun threads, leaving Marietta to sort the new batch of dye-producing flowers.

She spread the day's bounty atop the broad dining table, one whose size had been meant to serve far more than two lone women. As Marietta snipped and bundled the flowers, stems, and leaves into appropriate piles of green and yellow and rose, she idly glanced at the large loom in the corner, which was the only other piece of furniture to grace the dining room. As usual, the mere sight of the strings already secured in place, awaiting new threads to bring yet another pattern to life, filled her with a sense of satisfaction.

She had long since come to love the warp and the weft, the slow growth of a pattern as she passed the shuttle through the strings. She liked creating new patterns, new combinations of colors. She had enjoyed convincing Mr. Hissop to sell their goods, had thrilled to know a small success when he had ordered another delivery, had dared to hope for a brighter future when he nodded at the designs of lady's reticules she had sketched in proposal. She did not feel it immodest to acknowledge to herself that she and her aunt had snatched a future by the clever use of this machine, had designed possibilities from nothing.

But would it all turn to nothing? Assuming Lord Galbreth did not recover, was Mr. Westby the kind of man to simply cast them out, or to demand rent for his property?

Even if Galbreth did recover, might he suddenly wish he had no "entanglements" about the property? Marietta had not seen her aunt and Lord Galbreth together except in the most public of meetings, such as chapel, so she could not say from any real knowledge what depth of devotion Lord Galbreth felt toward her aunt. Either by Silvia's demand, or mutual choice, the two had kept their alliance very quiet and discreet. How did that bode for promises being kept?

And what was to keep new promises, those to his son, from being made?

Marietta closed her eyes and blew out a puff of breath, telling herself to quit attempting to sort out unanswerable questions.

"What's that?" Aunt Silvia said, startling Marietta, for she had not realized her aunt had returned inside the house. To judge from the handful of green-dyed wool in Silvia's hand, she must have hung out the new batch of thread to dry and was now prepared to comb yesterday's efforts, to ready the wool for spinning, as they did every afternoon.

"I am just a little weary," Marietta said, truthfully enough.

"Well then, sit and rest a spell. Leave those flowers, my girl, they'll keep. Come, you can tell me something."

"What is that?" Marietta asked as she took her aunt's suggestion and sat on the nearest chair.

"Tell me about Mr. Westby. I admit to a great curiosity about the prodigal son," Aunt Silvia said with a twinkle in her eye.

What was there to say? "He seems very . . . American."

Silvia placed a segment of wool atop one comb and began to scrape the two paddlelike combs against each other, currying the woolen threads into the condition that readied them for spinning. "What can you mean by 'very American'?" she asked.

Marietta frowned. "I do not know exactly. I do not know the man. It is just that he seems . . . so large, so *broad* in all ways. Not heavy, mind you, but all of a size!" She shrugged her shoulders, as if to shake loose a better description. "I only saw him for a minute or two, but, well, he seems to take up a great deal of space. I suppose that is what I mean by 'American.' He does not seem to me to be capable of . . . mincing, as some gentlemen we know care to do. Though, in fairness, Mr. Westby made me a credible leg."

Aunt Silvia considered this, a finger to her chin. "I daresay a credible leg is far to be preferred to mincing."

"Well, of course it is, but . . . I cannot quite seem to explain myself! It is something to do with the way he stands, the way he holds his head. It is his bearing, more than anything else. Although he is taller than some, I should venture to guess, it somehow seemed as if he would always be . . . dominant, even should a taller man stand beside him."

"How fanciful you are today, my dear! Perhaps he is merely high in the instep."

"Pompous? Perhaps. I could not say," Marietta said, but silently she thought that, no, that was not the word she would choose. *Commanding* perhaps, but for all the brevity of her conversation with Mr. Westby, she felt it might be unfair to label him pompous. Curious, that, for she had no reason to think benevolently upon the very man who could destroy her future.

She played with the pink ribbon tied just below her bosom. "I find myself hoping, should he inherit, that Mr. Westby will choose to be an absentee landlord. We might stay here in this house yet should he prove indifferent to the matter."

At her aunt's eloquent shrug, Marietta scowled at the ribbon already beginning to fray, and this her second-best gown. Perhaps she could afford a new ribbon to replace it, if all went well, by autumn. . . . "Oh, why must we wait upon some stranger's decision before we know if the worst is to occur or not!" she said the thought aloud.

"What choice do we have?" Aunt Silvia asked logically.

Marietta put back her shoulders, in a show of defiance as much as to regather her poise. "There is one other choice."

"What is that, dear?"

"We could go to Lord Galbreth, and in front of his son, have him swear the house is yours for the keeping."

Silvia's hands stilled. "Marietta," she chided softly, but with a stern edge hidden just beneath the words, "only think how that must look."

"I can understand your reluctance, but I could go alone. Lord Galbreth would understand—"

"No," Silvia said.

"But you are the one who has made me read *A Vindication of the Rights of Women*. You are the one who tells me, no matter how we women might try to manage a life for ourselves, we are ever the victim to male whims," Marietta stated.

"Oh, no, my dear girl!" Aunt Silvia gave her a stern look. "Do not think that you can cozen me by throwing my own words back at me! *I* am the Free Thinker among us two. You would look the very model of a hoyden, going to a man you scarcely know and making demands of him! Demands which, by the way, Aaron tells me are already satisfied. I know you have little reason to trust men, my dear girl, but I cannot allow you to do anything that could taint your reputation—"

"I would rather have no reputation than no home."

"Marietta!" Aunt Silvia said, with a rare and heavy censure.

Marietta set her chin in defiance, even as she stiffly stood to go and fetch another set of wool combs.

Just before she crossed the room's threshold, Marietta glanced back long enough to see that her aunt's chagrined alarm had begun to recede from her features. Aunt Silvia, no doubt, thought that was an end to the matter, but Aunt Silvia was mistaken.

Three

"So she changed your name," Lord Galbreth said to Fane, the words issued from between labored breaths.

Fane stood ten feet from the dying man's bed, gazing into a face that had a vestige of handsomeness to it yet, despite the wasting disease that was slowly claiming Lord Galbreth's life. The head of thick hair the man yet boasted was dark but graying, peeping out in tufts from under a winter wool sleeping cap, and the man's dark eyes were framed by lines, no doubt from a lifetime of scowling.

"If by 'she' you mean Mama, then, yes, she changed our surname to White," he answered.

"That's the reason I never found you! I never thought she'd stoop to such a common trick. Too high in her opinion of herself, I thought." Lord Galbreth wheezed before going on. "White! That is so ordinary a name a man could be excused for thinking it was taken by a criminal or an escapee."

"As I understand the situation, we *were* escapees."

"Oh, going to display a high dudgeon with me, are you?" Lord Galbreth gave a breathless laugh.

His eyes were shadowed by pain, but all the same keen with interest. He had recognized the ring at once, and had not needed to say it was one of the belongings Lady Galbreth had taken with her when she had disappeared. It had been proof enough of Fane's claims, even if Galbreth could not see with his own eyes his son's resemblance to himself.

"So, as you grew up being called Peter White, how is it you now call yourself Fane Westby?"

"Mama always called me Fane. I thought it a pet name." He felt himself coloring at what had been revealed as a life-long naiveté on his part. "It means 'glad or joyful.' "

"I know what it means. I named you thus, did I not?" his father said, sounding weaker, less gruff. Was this man capable of being softened by the emotion of the moment? Mama would have said no. She would have said it was all a ruse, to dupe you into trusting the man. "I'm only surprised I never found so little as a hint of your whereabouts, with such a name as Fane to distinguish you. I sent a man to America to look there, you know," Lord Galbreth wheezed.

"I did not allow the name to be commonly used."

"It was a pet name indeed then."

"Is this all we have to say to one another?" Fane said tersely. "Taunts? Mama always said—"

"Yes, what did she say of me? What taradiddles did she tell?" Lord Galbreth shuddered, as if convulsed by pain, but after a moment he gasped in a breath and went on. "Did she tell you that I was a monster? A wifebeater? A lout?"

Fane narrowed his eyes and nodded once. "Were you not?" he challenged.

The dying man grinned, the whiteness of his teeth almost the same shade as his too-pale skin. "I suppose

I was all those things," he said with no evident remorse. Lord Galbreth then lifted a hand to point a finger at Fane, his arms apparently lacking strength for he could only hold his hand aloft for a moment before it fell once more to the blankets covering him. "I will stand accused of some things, but one I will not. I have no doubt that woman—"

"Margaret. Her name was Margaret," Fane interrupted darkly.

"I have no doubt Margaret made me look the blackest of all blackguards. Though I will not say I have been a good man, I will have it known I have been largely fair." Lord Galbreth wheezed several breaths in and out, but his gaze remained solidly locked with Fane's until he regained the strength to go on. "I hit her. Once. It was no gentle thing. She was beyond stubborn, that one. I do not even remember what we fought over, but she would not let it go, and I thought to make her."

"She did not claim otherwise," Fane said, his jaw working. "But once was one time too many. You caused her tooth to darken—"

"Aye, I did. And in payment, she abandoned her marriage vows!" Lord Galbreth said, struggling up to balance on his elbows. He began to cough raggedly. The door leading from the hallway opened, and Lord Galbreth's valet peered in, his brows lifted in silent inquiry. Galbreth settled back against his pillows, and waved the valet away, his coughs lessening after a minute.

"You were cruel to strike her," Fane said flatly.

"She was crueler yet to take my son away!" the old man wheezed, and to Fane's surprise he saw tears well and spill down his father's cheeks. Tears of regret? Or did the man's eyes merely water from the force of his coughing? Lord Galbreth did nothing to wipe the tears away.

"How did she keep you both, boy? Did she marry again?" the dying man demanded, looking out from eyes as blue as Fane's own.

"How could she when she remained married to you?" Fane said, just keeping a snarl from entering his voice. He lifted his hand, making a sharp gesture. "Do not reply, for I might not be answerable for my actions if you were to disparage her! Suffice it to say that she never married, nor even allowed herself to be courted. For years I was told that my dead father had left her an income, but I later came to understand that she had sold her jewels when she first came to America. We lived all those years from the proceeds. We were not wealthy, but we had what we needed."

"*Her* jewels, eh?"

Fane put up his chin "The ones she brought into the marriage as dowry."

"Dowry indeed! That made them *my* jewels, you realize," his father said with an oddly droll twist to the cutting words. "One could argue that she stole them from me."

Fane's fist knotted at his sides. "If she took them without your permission, it was because you had first stolen her dignity."

"Oh, dignity! Yes, your mother had plenty of that! Enough for two women." Lord Galbreth paused to cough weakly, and even through the haze of his anger, Fane could see how the interview had begun to sap the man's limited strength.

"I was to pay for that sense of dignity she prized so highly, and pay dearly," his father went on. He then gave a shuddering breath, and when he turned his gaze upward again to meet Fane's, this time Fane was all but certain the tears brimming anew in the man's eyes were born of real emotion. The impression caused him to frown, and to unexpectedly experience a moment of sympathy.

"I have no other children, Fane. Not a son to read to me when the pain is beyond bearing. Not a daughter to wipe my brow in my fevered final days. I have been alone in this house all these years, four-and-twenty since your mother sailed away! I did not get to see you grow. I remember only a small infant, a tiny child who looked something like me—and, now, to see you grown—!"

Lord Galbreth coughed, without spirit, and the tears flowed. "I did not get to tell Margaret I was sorry. I would have, you know, I would have, and on my knees if she'd demanded it so! I have never struck another being since. I changed. But she never gave me a chance to prove I could." Lord Galbreth closed his eyes, but the tears flowed out from under the lids to streak downward to his pillow. "I was cruel, but she was crueler by far," he whispered.

Fane stared down at the weakened creature in the bed, the man's pain-filled words resounding in his head. He ought to deny it all, ought to call the man a liar, or a fool at best . . . but his father's pain was too sharp and seemed too unfeigned to dismiss so easily.

Too, as painful and uncomfortable as it was to admit it to himself, Fane had grown up knowing his mother was capable of harshness, of snap judgments, of grudges carried. Most of the time she had been a model of womanly virtues, tender and loving, but there had been times when a sudden assumption that she was being slighted or affronted had plunged them into the most awkward of social moments.

There had been the time she had thought the parson had cut her at a picnic—when it was revealed later that he had forgot his spectacles and had simply not seen her nod at him. A war of silence between them had lasted for months, even after an understanding of the facts had been revealed to her by friends.

And there was the time Fane had got in a bout of fisticuffs with Donnie Wilkins. Mama would not be in the same sewing circle with Mrs. Wilkins from that day forward, no matter that Fane insisted repeatedly that *he* had instigated the fight purely for the fun of scuffling with the larger boy.

There were a dozen more examples of sudden contentiousness that sprang to Fane's mind, and each of them pounded at the wall of truth as he had at long last been told it by his mama. Could it be his father was not the all-wicked, often-vicious creature of whom his mama had spoken when at last she had revealed his father was in fact living yet, and a wealthy landed Englishman?

Could it be that the man had truly changed, had chosen to improve the way he treated those around him? Was there another side to this man—this man whose name Fane had only known for the past dozen weeks?

Had Mama wronged her husband as much as she herself had been wronged by him?

Fane shuddered, torn by the pull of old loyalties

and new revelations, and remembered his mother's disclosures, made only because she knew she was dying. Following a logic of her own making and typical of her strong personality, after years of silence, Mama had decided her son's birthright was no longer to be denied him.

But the revelations she had made had also come with a warning: Fane was to remember, always, that his father had been a cruel man, capable of harming the very ones he ought to love. A barony could be Fane's one day—but only, he was made to swear, if he did not have to pay the price of his own happiness to obtain it.

"Give up the hope of the title, if you must! Don't stay overlong in Galbreth's company, or he'll charm you, make you begin to believe his lies. Return to America, or sell the rest of my jewels and travel as you please, but do not allow that man to rule you, to belittle you as he tried to do me!" Mama had pleaded between tears.

It was a bitter memory that when Mama had passed from this earth not three months ago, her last words had been a reminder that Fane had sworn not to be taken in by a charmer's tales should he venture to sail for England and seek his birthright.

And yet, when Fane was sorting out his mama's things and came again across the neatly printed card she had penned for him, listing the direction of Westby Hall in an area known as Kendall Town, outside London, her warnings had dimmed to mere shadows around the growing curiosity that her revelations had illuminated. Fane had a father! Not a lost-at-sea sailor long dead and gone, but a man living yet. Fane had always known his father had been English, but to learn he was of the landed gentry—a class frequently despised by the people he had grown to manhood among—was nearly as much a shock as the fact the man yet lived.

He had started to write to the address a dozen times, and lost a week's sleep before actually putting pen to paper and doing so, addressing the notice of his own existence to Aaron Westby, Lord Galbreth, care of Westby Hall.

Perhaps it was grief at the loss of his mother, at having no siblings, at having the foundations of his home crumble out from under him—but Fane had not waited the three or four months it would take for his letter to arrive and a response to return to America. As he had indicated in his letter to Lord Galbreth, he would see that his mother's stone was set in place in the Philadelphia cemetery, raise a sum of cash, store the house's few valuables, ask the neighbor to watch the house until his possible return, and then he would set sail at once.

Not quite a month later, Fane had taken leave of his employment, not telling them his destination nor even how long he might be away—and set sail for a country he had unknowingly left when only an infant. He had not wanted to wait for a rejection from this man who had fathered him. If he was to have one, or offer one himself, Fane wished it to be soon, and in person.

And now he stood at the foot of his father's death bed, and could only ponder where the truth lay. Was this Lord Galbreth a consummate actor, posturing and declaring his greater innocence? Or had Mama been too quick to judge, too willing to remember only the bad in this man?

"She was so cruel," Lord Galbreth repeated, the words ragged. "I have done my penance a hundred times over, my boy. But I can see you doubt me. You have no proof." Emotion raced across the man's face, a seeming demonstration of regret or sorrow. "I cannot blame you." Lord Galbreth closed his eyes, his chest shaking with silent tears that shortly turned to a bout of dreadful coughing.

Fane stood and watched, and wondered why the time must be so short, too short to come to know this man, to judge his father for himself—for he knew the rattle of a death cough and how little time it promised.

The cough quieted, and Fane looked up sharply, but although his father lay still, the eyes were opened and fixed keenly upon him. Steady, seeing eyes.

"What are you thinking, my boy?" Lord Galbreth asked.

Fane looked down for a moment, not having realized his emotions must be playing across his face. "It is just that you reminded me, for a moment, of someone." *Of Mama,* he did not say aloud. Whatever else Lord Galbreth was, this man had surely been her equal when it came to spirit. Perhaps two such strong souls never could have found happiness anyway, even if Mama had not taken fate into her own hands.

Fane folded his hands together before him and lifted his chin. "But let us speak to the obvious question. Since your man told me you had received my letter, I know my appearance here cannot be entirely a surprise to you. So I ask you—do you wish I had not come? That rather I had awaited your response?"

"No," Lord Galbreth answered at once. "I prayed you meant what you wrote, that you would come as soon as possible. You cannot imagine . . . it is enough just to see you again," he went on, but the words were muttered, as if he spoke more to himself than to Fane. He shook his head, coughed mildly, and said, "You are my heir. You are to inherit the estate, the title, everything. Tell me this pleases you."

Fane felt his mouth twist in consternation. "I cannot, sir. I will not pretend that I have given no thought to the possibility that, as your son, I might stand to inherit. But I tell you honestly that I do not know if I want any of this."

It was more than the threat of recognition that hung over Fane's head while he stood on English soil that drove his words, much more. Fane glanced about the room, the gesture taking in more than just the bed-chamber, but also the grandeur of the large house and grounds beyond these four walls. Such affluence, em-bedded as it was in the kind of pomp decried by every other mouth in America, was worlds away from what he had been raised amongst. And now it was promised to Fane, who had done nothing to earn it but to be born. How could he say it pleased him, when in truth his response was to be overwhelmed and baffled by the very idea?

His father eyed him with a kind of wary considera-tion. "Then what brought you here?" he asked at length.

Fane hesitated a moment, then spoke the simple truth. "To see you, sir."

"That is all? Not in hopes of the inheritance, eh?" Lord Galbreth questioned, his expression doubtful.

Fane could not know what showed in his own expression, but after a moment the doubt in Lord Galbreth's gaze melted away. He seemed to choke for a moment, and his lower lip quivered. "It is to be yours, by rights. Only this house is entailed, and the estate is free of all debt but the cost of keeping the sheep herds until the wool harvest and the time for slaughter. I dared to hope, all these years. . . . I built it up for you, Fane." Lord Galbreth's voice broke and became a cough. As though by force of will, he pushed down the cough, and repeated, "For you, my boy."

Fane said nothing, merely moving his hands to clasp them behind his back, for despite the endless days on the ship to think of the possibility, he was not quite able to conceive of the idea of one day inheriting a wealth he had never known was to be his.

He could see his father was growing weaker by the moment, and wondered if it were real emotion or playacting that so drained his strength.

"Perhaps I should allow you to rest now, sir," Fane suggested.

"No, no. I've time enough to rest in my grave! And do not give me that same censorious look the surgeon gives me," Lord Galbreth wheezed. "I can tell his physicking is doing me no good. 'Tis but a matter of time, and there's no point in pretending otherwise."

Fane had no response to make to that, so instead he cast about for a change of topic, something far less disturbing than talk of death. "Do you know, sir, that your property is being guarded by young ladies who ride about with pistols at the ready?"

"That would be Miss Hampton," his father said,

closing his eyes in apparent weariness, but offering a half-smile all the same.

Fane kept a new frown from forming, pulled despite himself by the appeal of that half-smile.

"Is she a tenant, sir?"

"Quite, quite! Lives with her aunt. But we'll see that's all settled."

"Settled?" Fane echoed.

The question was lost as his father succumbed to another coughing fit. When he recovered, Galbreth tapped the covers once with his forefinger. "Come, sit by me. Please."

"I should come back later—"

"No! Do not go, Fane, my boy," Lord Galbreth said, shaking his head with what little vigor was left to him. His eyes glittered like those of a man with a fever. "I wish to ask something of you."

Fane stiffened, wondering if the terrible Lord Galbreth of his mother's tales was now to show his true self, the aspect Fane had been made to expect from the man.

"I must know . . . please," Lord Galbreth went on. "The thing of it is. . . . May I call you 'son'?" The question was hesitantly asked, and Fane sensed in surprise that it had cost the man in pride to say it.

Despite his mama's warnings, a part of him warmed at that hesitancy, at that show of humility. Where was the smooth-talking monster he had expected to meet? Or was this the monster's trick, to hide his real intent behind seeming emotion?

Yet, even so, how to deny such a reasonable request? What did the man stand to gain by fooling Fane anyway?

In the final accounting, Galbreth's reasons did not matter anyway. Fane did not need this man's blessing, nor his money. He had skills, abilities, and good honest employment awaiting his return, should he choose to go home to America. He could make his way in life, there, if not in this unfamiliar land. In America he could take on again the persona by which he was known, Peter White—and on that soil he need not fear the name could mean his imprisonment.

"May I call you son?" Lord Galbreth repeated, his gaze fixed and anxious.

Fane stared into that gaze, and worked hard to keep any expression from crossing his own features. Could he bear to allow this man, this stranger, to call him son? In what way had this man earned the right?

Yet, could Fane be so cruel as to disallow a dying man's simple wish?

It was, after all, only a name, a title, and did not make him this man's son in any important way . . . and had not his own soul thrilled to learn there was a man breathing yet whom he could call "father?" Had it not been gratifying to learn his mother's pet name for him was something more, that it had resonance beyond what Fane had ever as a lad imagined it might? Was it so impossible to believe this man was equally moved to learn his son was found?

Slowly Fane gave a brief nod. "You may," he agreed, not quite able to keep his tone utterly neutral, for even to his own ears he sounded stiff.

Lord Galbreth's mouth twitched, and Fane realized the man smiled through a new bout of tears. He looked away, discomfited by the sight.

"Son," Lord Galbreth said, and Fane looked up to

see the man had stretched out a hand. "Will you come to my side? Will you sit with me?" As he had sat at his mother's side as her heart slowly gave out? This was too much to ask, too intimate a request between strangers. . . .

The outstretched hand wavered, and a sheen of sweat broke out on the dying man's forehead. Despite its quaver, the hand remained outstretched.

Fane's gaze slid to a portrait that hung beside the bed, a painting he had seen upon first entering. It had shocked him, for he'd had no idea that it had been painted. It was obviously of Lord Galbreth, four-and-twenty years younger, and on his lap, supported by his arm, rested a chubby infant, its face very like that in a miniature his mother had kept by her bed; the infant, Fane knew, could be none other than himself.

He lowered his gaze from the portrait, frowning down at his own boots, as if they were somehow the cause of his continuing paralysis.

But then his feet moved, almost as if of their own volition, and they carried him across to the bed, and in a moment Fane had sat atop the blankets.

He slowly took up his father's hand, not quite wanting to, but another part of him had no inclination to move away, not even when Lord Galbreth repeatedly whispered his name in tearful gratitude.

Four

It was only a matter of hours later that the village surgeon closed his medical bag and shook his head in regret, as Lord Galbreth's valet pulled the sheet over the dead man's face.

Fane vaguely noted that somewhere in the distance sheep had already started to bleat, as if greeting the dawn that was just beginning to lighten the room's black shadows to grey. The stirring of life without the house seemed incongruous with the death within.

"That old man had an iron will," Doctor Hammill said with a surgeon's resigned sigh.

"So I have been told," Fane answered, his head lowered, his hands crossed behind his back.

"I believe he was waiting on your arrival. You should take comfort from that thought."

Fane merely grunted, his throat momentarily blocked by a sudden keen sense of loss for what might have been.

"Please accept my regrets, my lord."

Fane lifted his head. " 'My lord'?" he repeated, shaking his head at the appellation.

"I cannot pretend to know the components of your father's will, nor if at any time he had seen to it that you were legally declared dead. . . ."

Fane lifted his eyebrows at the suggestion.

"—Yes, well," the doctor went on, "but as Lord Galbreth always hoped that you would be found, it is to be presumed you are now the fifth Baron Galbreth." He hefted his bag in preparation of leaving.

Fane frowned, for it was one thing to have pondered the thought of inheriting land and wealth and a title, and another altogether to be hailed by that title. In America, should he return to the place he had always considered home, there was one faction who might be expected to fawn over this change in his lot, and another who would as soon spit at his boots as call him "my lord." Unfortunately, if this title was indeed his, there were far too few of the kind of Americans who fell somewhere in-between.

And where did his own opinion fall in the matter?

"I have no doubt that Poole will have a knowledge of your father's business, and how to contact his solicitors," the doctor suggested helpfully.

Fane nodded, aware that Poole was . . . had been his father's butler. "I suppose he is my butler now," Fane murmured.

"My lord?" The doctor leaned toward him with a slight frown to indicate he had not heard.

"Nothing. I mean to say, yes, thank you. It was very good of you to come so late last night." He put out his hand to shake. The doctor seemed a trifle nonplused, as he began to bow over the gesture before he stopped himself and shook Fane's hand instead.

"It is the custom in America," Fane explained, faintly annoyed to have again forgotten these European fellows preferred a bow to a handclasp. One would think he might have learned the lesson during his voyage to England, especially as he had received the cut more than once for his forgetfulness. It was curious that a bow from the waist or an inclination of the head was considered more polite behavior than an honest grasp—but then again, not so curious if one did not subscribe to the revolutionary concept of equality among the classes. After all, bowing allowed one to avoid touching those one did not deign to touch.

"I am afraid you must either send me an accounting of your charges, or else perhaps Poole can see to your fee," Fane added, once again at a loss of how to go on. He presumed the butler had access to funds by which to pay the everyday expenses of such a large household, but he did not know that for a fact.

"Certainly, my lord." The doctor reached for his hat, seemingly undisturbed by this arrangement, so Fane must not have stepped too far afield with the suggestion. "Do you wish me to stop at the vicarage and inform the rector of your father's passing?" the doctor kindly inquired.

Fane closed his eyes, as much from the emotional weight of the question as his physical exhaustion. It had been a long uncertain voyage, only to end in a long night at a dying man's side. Fane opened his eyes, and shook his head. "No, thank you. I will have to see the rector anyway to arrange the funeral."

"Of course. Do you have the rector's direction?"

Fane shook his head again, and listened to the doctor's description of how to find his way.

After the doctor left, Fane was tempted to turn back, to look again at the unmoving figure on the bed, but there were no more answers or explanations to be had of the late Lord Galbreth. Instead Fane slipped from the room, closing the door behind him. He leaned against its solid length, heaved a long sigh, and realized he had already half-forgotten the directions the doctor had given him. He should have written them down, only he'd had no notion of where to find paper and ink. In fact, he had no notion of how to find anything in this house, not even the room readied for him, for he had spent the entire afternoon and night with his father. For that matter, short of the road before the house, he had no idea even of the countryside, of the land in which he found himself.

All he did know was that he was now more alone than when he had first stepped off the ship from America.

At the sound of a step on the path that ran before the house, Marietta looked up from where she had just drawn the front door closed behind her. She expected to see Mr. Hissop's shop lad, come to fetch an ordered new shawl or other woolen item, but to her surprise a man strode along the path. He was not just any man, either, for she recognized him at once as the tall, broad-shouldered gentleman who called himself Fane Westby. To her chagrin, here was the son of the man she had determined—despite her aunt's prohibitions—to call upon this very morning.

Marietta quickly reached to knot the ribbons of her bonnet, pleased to be discovered otherwise properly adorned this time, complete with bonnet, gloves, and a shawl tied about her shoulders. She suspected a touch of color filled her cheeks at the memory of having been previously caught without a hat, as well as with flowers she had woven in her plait in a fanciful moment, no doubt making her look like quite the hoyden. At least she had been wearing riding gloves that had hid her flower-stained fingers from his sight.

Her movement must have captured his attention, for he came to a stop at the end of the graveled walk that branched toward her home from the wider village path. He gave her a nod of acknowledgment, which compelled one from her as well.

She forced herself to hide a frown of anxiety at his appearance here. Did he come as his father's representative, bent on casting them out? Had she left the matter of putting her arguments to Lord Galbreth too late? Was it possible the son already exercised influence over the father's decision in the matter of the house?

"Mr. Westby?" she inquired, her voice not quite steady.

"Miss Hampton, is it not?" he inquired, frowning mildly, in the manner of one whose attention is divided.

At her nod, he bowed and she curtsied, and she became aware that he did not sport a hat, as though he had left the house in a great hurry, and that he wore no overcoat as well. Peculiar! The day was bright but not especially warm, for even the thick woolen shawl she wore knotted before her bosom was scarcely enough to keep away a chill. What could have brought him out of doors in such obvious haste?

She was aware she began to play with the beaded fringe of her shawl in what must look the nervous dis-

play it was. She was also aware her eyes were opened
too wide and her voice had come out a little too high.

"You live here?" Mr. Westby motioned toward the
small house behind her.

"Yes." She was glad she wore her best gown and
finest shawl—a show of finery might somehow make
it easier to defy him, or plead with him, or cajole him
into granting her and her aunt the privilege of keeping the house.

Mr. Westby's gaze became more focused as he
looked to the small but finely appointed dwelling behind her. There were many windows to reveal the fine
silk curtains within, and Marietta knew the delicate
and charming pieces of furniture that did not belong
to her nor her aunt, but rather to the Westby family,
must be at least somewhat visible from the path as well.

"Is this the dower house?" he asked.

"Yes," Marietta answered shortly.

Her aunt, greying hair pulled into a simple knot at
the back of her head, opened the door. "Marietta?"
she inquired from the doorway. "Have we a caller?"

"Yes, Aunt Silvia," Marietta turned to her to say,
glad for an ally in this moment fraught with tension.
"The gentleman I was telling you about has come."
She turned back to Mr. Westby, saying in a falsely tran-
quil tone, "Aunt Silvia, this is Mr. Westby. Mr. Westby,
may I present my aunt, Miss Nicholson."

Mr. Westby bowed to Silvia, who curtsied in return.
When Mr. Westby rose, he made an apologetic gesture
with his hand. "Excuse me for disturbing you, but I
think I must be lost," he said. "I am in need of further
directions. I was told to pass by the dower house, which
I now discover I have found, but after that I am un-

certain of the way." He paused a moment, then said, "I confess I did not realize the place would be occupied."

Marietta felt her shoulders relax, for how could he have come to order them out if he did not know they lived here?

"Am I right to continue along this way if I am to find the rectory?" he asked, pointing to the right.

"Oh, yes," Marietta said, relieved at this further evidence of a reprieve.

Aunt Silvia, wearing a dress far older than Marietta's and covered in spots, all of them of varying hues, left the doorway to come to Marietta's side. She wiped her hands—hands currently stained a mottled green—on a piece of linen, and gazed up at the much taller Mr. Westby. "May I ask, sir, how does Lord Galbreth go on?" she asked, and Marietta heard the note of worry in her aunt's tone. Could Mr. Westby hear it, too?

His lips came together for a moment to form a grim line. "I regret to say that Lord . . . that my father passed away early this morning," Mr. Westby said.

Both women gasped aloud, and Aunt Silvia went pale as she pressed a hand to her mouth.

"But I was just going to call on him!" Marietta blurted, then wished she had not for the sharp, pained glance Aunt Silvia sent her. Not that it now would matter that Silvia guessed Marietta had meant to plead for a document that showed the house was theirs to keep, for Aaron, Lord Galbreth, could no longer swear out such a document.

If Aunt Silvia was annoyed, that irritation however was lost to a greater emotion. After a long stunned moment Silvia gasped out, "Our regrets to you,

Mr. . . . Or, I suppose it is not 'Mr. Westby' now," she said through stiff lips. "But only listen to me babbling on! Please accept my regrets, my lord. The happy news is that you were there with him at the end. I know it was Aaron's dearest wish that his son should be found . . . !"

Aunt Silvia at last turned her gaze from his, blinking rapidly, not letting the tears yet fall, but unable to keep the despair from her features. "Pardon me," she murmured, and turned at once and stepped briskly toward the house.

Marietta moved forward a step, keenly aware that Mr. Westby stared after Aunt Silvia with a puzzled frown tilting his brows.

"Indeed, my lord, you have our regrets and our prayers. Lord Galbreth, that is, the former Lord Galbreth . . . he was . . . he was very often kind to us," she said softly, wondering once again what this sad turn of events signified for their future.

"Thank you, Miss Hampton." An expression that might be deemed regret turned down the corners of his mouth for a brief moment, but then he gave one quick nod and glanced off to the right, expressionless. "I must arrange the ceremony with the rector," he said, explaining his destination.

"Oh, yes, of course," Marietta murmured in understanding. It was only reasonable that the man suffered from the shock of a sudden death, and it would explain his having come away from the house in such an incomplete mode of dress.

"You have but to stay on the path," she indicated the direction. "It leads over that hillock, and curves back toward the village, you see. Stay to the right at the oak, and that will take you directly to Rector Manning's garden. You must feel free to make use of the gate and approach his rear door—I am afraid his front door has stuck fast since last year's rainstorms.''

Mr. Westby nodded again, the morning sun gilding his brown hair with a halo of gold. The sight of it struck Marietta mute, and despite the rudeness of it, she found herself staring. But it was something more than merely the play of light that caught at her; there was something about Mr. Westby that fixed one's gaze upon him. He was large, as his father was . . . had been. He had a well-shaped head sitting atop a sturdy neck, and she could see with an artistic eye that even though his size came from muscle and bone rather than corpulence, his waistcoat would take a measure more fabric to construct than might an average man's. Too, there was something about his hatless state, the missing overcoat—the lack of the usual outdoor trappings made him seem, well, foreign. Even his accent caught at her this morning. His was a blend of English and American tones, no doubt the result of being raised by an English mother who, it seemed clear now, had fled to the former Colonies. Altogether, he was the sort of man one simply could not overlook.

"Thank you for the directions," he said, breaking Marietta's reverie as he gave her a nod in preparation of leaving.

"Of course," she said, returning the nod. "My lord," she added abruptly, causing him to turn back toward her. She knew it was not the best of times to speak, but she was also aware that, with Lord Galbreth gone, her fate and Aunt Silvia's was all the more tenuous. "I. . . ."

She almost brought up the issue of the house and its ownership, but she could not, the words being too gauche, too soon after Lord Galbreth's death, to pass her lips. Instead she said somewhat lamely, "I hope it might be acceptable to you, my lord, should we call upon you later to more properly pay our condolences."

"Of course." He nodded, but a look of weariness crossed his face, reminding her that Silvia had said his mother was dead. How long ago had Lady Galbreth been deceased? To judge by the drawn look of his features, not long. A flash of sympathy coursed through Marietta, and she thought she rather liked Mr. Westby for this show of feeling—for if nothing else it seemed to imply he could not be a wholly callous man. Surely that bode well for her future dealings with the man.

He did not turn at once to move away. Instead he glanced about, taking in the dower house, the surrounding trees, the fields that stretched away from where they stood in the dappled sunlight. "But I should warn you, Miss Hampton, if you wish to call upon me, perhaps it should be soon," he said in a quiet voice.

"Yes?" she questioned. This was very much to her liking. The sooner the better to call on him and put her case before him, for the suspense of not knowing her fate was an agony better not borne long.

He brought his gaze to meet hers directly, all vagueness erased, and he surprised her with a bittersweet smile. "For you see, my good lady, I do not know if I care to stay here long. Not long at all."

She stared. "You would return to America?"

He nodded once.

"And let a steward see to the property for you?" she asked in growing eagerness, one she was half-afraid he heard in her tone.

He gave her an unfathomable look. "What I might well do is refuse the inheritance altogether."

She felt her lips part in surprise, and she had to snap them closed and blink several times before she found her voice again, and then it was only to utter, "Oh?"

He inclined his head, turning the assent into a half-bow. "Good day, Miss Hampton," he said rather abruptly, perhaps regretting speaking so freely.

"Good day, my lord," she said, returning a curtsy.

She watched as he turned and strode away up the path in the direction she had indicated, so stunned that it was a few moments before she thought of her manners and ceased to stare after him. Great heavens! Would this man be so rash as to turn aside an inheritance of land and wealth?

And why did the thought of it bring her no peace? Was it just that she would know the same fears with the cousin who stood to inherit in Fane Westby's stead?

To herself she admitted she hoped she had seen some flickers of feeling, a possibility of compassion, in Mr. Westby's manners.

"Better the devil you know than the one you do not," she said aloud as she took a few steps down the path, only to stop abruptly. Her morning's outing had become pointless; she had no one on whom she needed to make a call, now that she knew the old Lord Galbreth was gone.

Lord Galbreth was dead; long live the new Lord Galbreth, she thought to herself . . . but who would that turn out to be?

Five

"Tell me your name again?" Fane asked the valet who had just shown him to his room.

"Bintliff, my lord."

"Call me sir."

"My lord?"

"I would prefer you call me just 'sir.' No 'my lord,' " Fane stated firmly. He had always known that refusing the inheritance was an option, but not until he had said it aloud to Miss Hampton had Fane really given the idea the weight it deserved. It felt false to allow others to call him 'my lord,' given the circumstances. "Sir will suit me just fine."

"As you wish. Sir," Bintliff said with a puzzled air.

"As to that other matter you mentioned . . . ," Fane said.

Bintliff looked up at him eagerly, disproving Fane's notion as to the average English valet being staid and unemotional. Or perhaps that was the butler's role? Certainly Bintliff did not seem to mind in the least allowing his sentiments to show on his face. Like now, for instance, it was easy to see Bintliff meant to offer his condolences.

"Sir, may I say how much I shall miss your father? He was a good man, and treated us servants well and fairly. I couldn't have asked for better employment, sir." Bintliff looked down at the floor, perhaps to give himself time to master a slight quaver that had come into his voice. When he looked up again, there was still regret poised in his eyes. "Not to be indelicate, sir, but I have to ask. May I assume I am to be retained as your valet, my . . . sir?"

"Well . . . see here, my good man, I do thank you for your kind words, and it is not that I have any objection to your services, but, the thing of it is . . . ," at the man's eager look, Fane found his denial faltered. He took a deep breath, and decided to just say his piece. "The truth is I have never before had a valet, and am not at all sure I shall be requiring one."

Bintliff's eyes grew round. "Never had a valet, sir? But! But!" the smaller man sputtered, and blinked several times as if he had just sustained a blow. "But surely they have valets in America, sir?"

"Of course they do—those who care for such trappings and can afford them do anyway."

Bintliff absorbed this information. "But, however have you managed? I assure you, my lord," he forgot the prohibition against the title as he warmed to his subject, "that with your new responsibilities, you will be far too occupied to concern yourself with the care of your garments, or your boots! And who would cut your hair, needless to say shave you in the morning? And I assure you I am an absolute master of the cravat—"

Fane held up a hand. "Enough! Let me be direct with you, for you must understand there is every possibility that I will be leaving England, Bintliff."

"Ah!" the valet replied, and then a peculiar look

crossed his face. "I quite understand. But may I ask my lord a question?"

"Of course," Fane said, shrugging out of his coat.

Bintliff reached at once to assist him. "As to your proposed travels, may I ask, would we be bound for America, or perhaps India? I understood from the letter I read aloud to your father, that you have been a merchant tradesman involved in the purchase of coffee, who sometimes sailed to far climes—"

"Bintliff," Fane interrupted, unsure whether to be annoyed or amused.

"Sir?"

"I meant that if I choose to leave England, it will be alone."

At the crestfallen look that overcame the short, tidy, black-haired servant, Fane quickly added, "I will, of course, write a glowing reference for you before I leave."

"Very good, sir," Bintliff said, managing to sound properly grateful, if only just, as he carefully folded Fane's coat over his arm.

Fane, curiously feeling as though he had just received a deserved scolding, motioned to the room around them. "My belongings are already put away?"

"Of course," Bintliff said on a sniff, and the tone of insulted injury made Fane smile briefly, even as he sighed to himself. He put both hands to his face, rubbing the skin as though he could rub away his exhaustion.

"Thank you," he said, letting his hands drop. "Might I request one other favor?"

"It is my pleasure to do any task my lord requires."

Fane smiled to himself, aware "my lord" was a sobriquet with which he would just have to learn to live . . . at least so long as he remained in England.

"I can think of nothing I should like so much as a bath," Fane said on a heartfelt sigh.

"Oh, certainly, my lord! In point of fact, if you will but step into the adjoining chamber, you will find I have already anticipated such a request."

"Bintliff," Fane gave in, now silently laughing wryly to himself. "I should be very gratified if, while I remain in England, you were to serve as my valet." After all, the man meant to do the job whether solicited or not.

"Of *course*, my lord!" Bintliff's chest puffed with satisfaction as he led the way to the adjoining room. "A bath seemed only logical, given your time aboard ship all these weeks. Travel is such a burden! And shipboard bathing is disagreeable at best. I already have a kettle before the fire in your room, should the water have cooled too much already and not be sufficiently to your liking, my lord. Er, that is, sir."

" 'My lord,' Bintliff. I concede the matter."

"Very good, my lord!"

Fane let the man's easy chatter about bathing preferences wash over him, even as he allowed the fellow to help him disrobe. It was probably just as well he was too weary to protest the unique experience of having someone else unbutton his sleeves, strip off his boots, and carry away his things after he stripped them off, for certainly Bintliff saw nothing amiss in tending to his new "master." Besides, having lived months at a time aboard a series of ships over the years, Fane knew there were some forms of nudity to which the human eye could choose to be blind, accepting it as no more than a reality of existence.

As Fane reclined in the bath—a luxuriously lengthy one, not a hipbath—he pushed aside thoughts of his father, not yet four hours gone, and listened for a moment to Bintliff's largely one-sided conversation (currently something about having added sandalwood scent to the water) before interrupting. "Bintliff, tell me about this place."

"This place? Do you mean Kendall Town, my lord?"

"Let us leave that for later. What I really mean is Westby Hall. The house. The estate. Its people."

"Oh yes, certainly. You will want to meet the entire staff, naturally, but it might serve you well to know something of them beforehand. Quite right, quite right," the valet clucked as he soaped a cloth with a cut block of soap.

Fane nodded, dipping his chin in the warm bath water and making ripples that spread slowly toward his toes. "Most specifically, I wish to know something of the women who live in the dower house."

Bintliff nodded. "Our dearly departed lord's mistress, and her niece," he supplied.

Fane sat up straight in surprise. "His *mistress?*"

Bintliff opened his mouth, and shut it again before going on, looking abashed. "It was the old lord's secret, my lord. Discretion was of the utmost importance—for the lady to maintain her standing in the community, of course, my lord. Only the niece and I know the absolute truth of it. Forgive me for revealing it so bluntly, but I presumed you ought to know." He stepped forward and stretched the soapy cloth toward Fane.

Fane accepted the cloth, even as he pondered the

fact that his father's lover lived not five minutes' walk from the estate house.

His father had taken a mistress? And why not? It was only logical that a man whose wife had left him should seek solace elsewhere. Then a disturbing thought struck Fane. "Tell me this, Bintliff. Can it be that Miss Hampton could be a half-sister to me?"

"Oh no, my lord," Bintliff said with a quick shake of his head. "She truly is Miss Nicholson's niece. She arrived in Kendall Town but three months past."

"Why? Is she orphaned?"

"No, her parents live yet." Bintliff narrowed his eyes for a moment, as if trying to gauge how Fane might respond to additional information. "I am afraid I can only repeat gossip as to why she lives with her aunt."

Fane eyed the valet in return. "Normally I have no liking for gossip."

The little valet seemed to approve the response. "I have a liking for it, my lord, I confess, but only for receiving it. I never deal it out."

"Then why would anyone care to share their tales with you?" Fane asked, not bothering to hide his skepticism.

"I have a sympathetic ear," Bintliff said, then grinned again. "I know when to cluck, when to shake my head, and when to murmur something that sounds like agreement."

Fane laughed aloud, beginning to like the valet in spite of himself. "So, I order you now, repeat the gossip you heard of Miss Hampton."

"I have not heard much, my lord. There was some manner of scandal, though. Her father sent her off, and word is he's not likely to take her back." He shook his head, as though in regret. "It must've been something, though, for as kind and gentle as the aunt is, still 'tis difficult to fathom why a loving papa would banish his daughter to live with such a one."

"Such a one?"

"Her aunt, Miss Nicholson—that's the elder of the two ladies, you see—now, they say she's a Free Thinker. Nonconformist—or at least that's what our rector calls some of these eccentric types."

"Ah," Fane said, then reached to scrub his face with the cloth, to mask the frown forming there. So, Miss Nicholson was of the eccentric mold, eh? A woman peculiar enough in her thinking to resist Society's dictates as to behavior. Was it a punishment for the niece to be sent to her . . . or had Miss Hampton been sent there because she was of the same ilk as the aunt?

Fane knew something of women with strong wills, of women who chose their own way despite the role Society said they must play. He knew better than to dismiss a woman's propensity, particularly if her propensity was to create complications.

What had his father said of the ladies in the dower house? *We'll see that's all settled.* All *what* was settled? *Settled* implied a difficulty that needed to be smoothed— what manner of difficulty? And who had he meant by "we?" Himself and Fane? Himself and a solicitor of the law, perhaps?

"Bintliff," Fane sputtered, after splashing his face free of soap, "is there aught else I should know about those two ladies?"

Bintliff thought a moment—and his very pause to think relieved some of Fane's concern. "You may care to know that the young lady has a beau, sir."

Fane gave a snort. "I am not asking about them because I am interested in pursuing Miss Hampton, if that is what you are thinking, Bintliff."

"Very good, my lord."

"I was merely curious to know why we have strangers living here among us. The knowledge that Miss Nicholson was my father's mistress makes sense of the matter, however, as a man would wish his lover to be near at hand."

"Quite, my lord."

"It was as well the affair was kept quiet, for the niece's sake," Fane mused as he scrubbed his knee.

"It was very discreet, my lord, even after the old lord and Miss Nicholson needed to meet here," Bintliff said as he dipped a finger into the water. "More hot water, my lord?"

Fane nodded absently. "Needed to meet here?"

"They could scarcely, er, be together in the dower house once the niece came to live there," Bintliff said, sounding as though he were repeating someone else's choice of words—undoubtedly those of Fane's papa. "More scent?" the valet suggested.

Fane nodded absently, lost to curious thoughts that his father had taken a mistress and that he had taken steps to assure that the lady's standing in the community remained unbesmirched by scandal. While the one act could be called ignoble, the other just the opposite. Of course, his father could have been discreet entirely for his own reasons—but why? He'd had nothing to lose, should word have got about, for everyone knew his wife was many years missing. Who could have blamed Lord Galbreth for taking a lover? No, the discretion had been solely to benefit the lady.

Suddenly Fane was glad he had come, glad he was to have a chance to know something of what his father really had been like, glad to discover that the man who had sired him had been seemingly something more than just a brutish boor.

"He must have loved her," Fane said the surprising thought aloud. "That woman . . . Miss Nicholson."

"I believe that to be a correct statement, sir," Bintliff said, having returned to the bathing room, carrying the heavy kettle before him by a cloth-wrapped handle. The valet poured a measure of the steaming contents into the space from which Fane moved his feet.

"So why did my father never have my mother declared legally dead, that he might marry Miss Nicholson? It makes no sense!"

"I was under the impression that even had he been free to marry her, Miss Nicholson was not of a mind to have him, my lord."

"Whyever not? It would have benefited her enormously."

Bintliff shrugged. "I did say she is an eccentric."

Fane stirred the water, spreading the added heat. "And a Free Thinker. I begin to believe you are most correct on that score. Extraordinary!"

"But the niece, Miss Hampton, she is all one could wish, so far as I can see. Clever, too. It is not generally known, but she founded a weaving business that she and her aunt conduct."

"Weaving? As on a loom?"

"Exactly, sir. The items they make are sold in the village by Mr. Hissop the merchant, and so most people have no idea who weaves them. Well, even if they suspect, they turn a blind eye to it, not wanting to acknowledge that the ladies might be engaged in trade—no doubt perceiving the income is how the ladies survive, I daresay."

"Did my father not provide for their income?" Fane asked in surprise.

"No, sir. Miss Nicholson has a small income, and Mr. Teedle, the local banker that is, sir, tells me that Miss Hampton has a very small monthly allowance as well, but Miss Nicholson has never accepted money or trinkets from Lord Galbreth."

"A mistress not accept money? Whoever heard of such a thing? I thought that was the point of being a mistress."

Bintliff gazed down at Fane, and together the two of them said, "An eccentric!"

"Indeed," Fane said. He shook his head before he gripped his nose with two fingers. He took a deep breath and then lay back in the tub so that the water washed over his head. His father had provided nothing for the ladies? *We'll see that's all settled,* he had said. Could that "settlement" be what Miss Hampton had meant to see his father about this morning? Did the niece possess the sense the aunt lacked—if not the curious show of pride? Had Miss Hampton meant to ask for money? She had paled when she had learned of his father's death—was that because she'd known it would distress her aunt . . . or because she'd seen an opportunity for financial advancement had slipped away?

Fane reared up out of the water to take a gulp of fresh air, shaking the water from his eyes, not liking the bend of his thoughts. What did he know of Miss Hampton anyway? That she was comely in her own way was irrelevant—many a comely woman could be devious or grasping. Admit it; even his own lovely mama had shown a misguided streak when it came to judging others, and sometimes her judgments had proved disastrous. He had only to look at his own childhood to see the truth of that.

So who was Miss Hampton? He had seen her in two guises: once with flowers in her hair, like a veritable gypsy, and once adorned in a modish ensemble that could have graced even the finest parlors in Philadelphia. Was she an adventuress? Why had her family shunned her? What had her "sin" been? What could cause a family to cast out their daughter . . . other than, of course, the old iniquity of wrongful carnal knowledge? But Bintliff thought the lady to be "all one could wish." The valet would have heard any tales of illicit sexuality. Certainly if a babe were on the way, Miss Hampton's intervening three month retirement from London would have led to an obvious display of that fact . . . unless her "sin" had been discovered at once instead of the usual two months later?

But besides a tidy waistline Fane had viewed for himself, Miss Hampton seemed strong, assured, and perhaps a little proud—not the hallmarks of a woman who has something to hide or who has done something wrong. Or at least, not one who will admit to having done wrong, he corrected himself, thinking again of his own mama.

But, more to the point was the fact that Miss Hampton lived in the dower house. Whether she was an honest woman or a strumpet in disguise, and whether he returned to America or stayed in England, at some level he would have to decide how best to "settle" the fact that two ladies not of his family resided on the estate.

He could, he supposed, leave the matter to whomever inherited the estate in his stead. Curious, though, how the thought of leaving the fate of the eccentric Miss Nicholson and her even more curious niece in the hands of some remote stranger—a cousin whose name Fane had never even heard—lay unsettled on his shoulders.

Perhaps that was because he had begun to perceive that here was a chance for him to lend his father a service, a first and final payment for Fane's very existence, and—he had to admit to himself—for his father's caring all these years about the child he had never been permitted to raise. After all, why should yet two more people be harmed by the debacle of Fane's parents' marriage?

He stepped out of the bath as Bintliff handed him a large, warmed towel to wrap around himself, and another with which to dry his hair. Fane moved to the bedchamber to stand before the roaring fire there, noting idly that the flames danced and weaved, seeming almost to mimic the sudden and recent shifts in his life. The dance of the Fates, as it were—but Fane considered that it had not been Fate that had brought him to this strange land, but rather his own actions. Despite anything else, despite learning his beginnings had been something other than he had always been told before, he was determined that from here forward he would be master to his own fate, would make his own choices.

In that moment, Fane decided he would stay here in England, at least long enough to see to the matter of the ladies in the dower house. He would not allow the possibility of encountering the one man who could identify him as a renegade drive him from this land—not before he had decided whether or not the ladies' presence was a boon or a bane to the estate. It was difficult to believe two ladies could pose any threat to either the estate or the memory of Fane's papa. Then again the one lady, his father's mistress, was an eccentric, and the other woman had been banished from her parents' home. Their presence here was, at best, suspect.

Yes, it behooved Fane to discover whether or not these peculiar tenants ought to be allowed to remain. Along with seeing to the fact that his father was properly interred, it would be the last service he could grant to the sire he'd not had time to come to know.

Of course, he could do nothing until the contents of his father's will were known. His father had said he was to inherit, so Fane had to assume the prospect had been legally set in place—but he would not count the inheritance as fact until he read it for himself. And the document might well specify what was to be done concerning either the ladies or the dower house.

No doubt the reading of the will could be achieved in short order. Poole, the butler, could perhaps advise Fane as to the direction of Father's solicitors, that the contents of the will might be the sooner revealed.

And if in the meanwhile Fane discovered a reason why the will's stated intentions must be broken, he would stay in England long enough to see to that as well.

"I should discover who this cousin might be, the soldier," he said aloud to himself. "The one who might inherit in my place." He would locate a copy of DeBrett's, to learn the man's name. Poole could tell him how to hire an investigator to ascertain something of the cousin's character, as Fane could scarcely travel to a Russian battlefield, in the midst of the British war against France, to discover the man's character for himself.

Fane began to hum, and smiled to himself a little at this sure sign of his own satisfaction with his decisions. It was gratifying to have defined a sense of purpose, something that could occupy his attention while he sojourned in this land of his birth. He would make his journey serve a dual purpose. The original one of seeing and becoming acquainted with his father had proved too fleeting—now he would see how best he might arrange matters before he left them behind him once more.

Once Fane was dry and robed in a sleeping gown, and his head laid down on one of the unfamiliar pillows in this unfamiliar room, it was no more than a minute before he was lost to dreams. Vague dreams of the tree-covered hills of America somehow becoming rolling green hills of pasture and hedgerows. Even in his sleep he wondered how he could be in both places at once.

Six

Marietta turned toward the dismal gray light that crept through the window, even though its somber color was scarcely more uplifting than the sight of Aunt Silvia dressed all in black. They had less than half an hour until the funeral services would begin for the former Lord Galbreth. Although it was fitting that the June day should be overcast and dreary, it too closely echoed the disheartening tone of Marietta's thoughts, and she wished for sunlight and warmth for Aunt Silvia's sake. She counted the peals of the distant parish church bells: three, on to six, and continuing to nine peals, the number announcing the fact that the deceased had been a man, rather than a child or a woman. Any of the curious who had not already heard of Lord Galbreth's death might guess it from the doleful sound. The mourners would already be gathering at the churchyard.

"Do you have some extra kerchiefs in your reticule?" Aunt Silvia asked, tears already teetering on her lashes.

"I do," Marietta turned from the window to assure her softly. "Are you ready?"

Aunt Silvia squared her shoulders. "I think I am. I must not make a fuss, I keep telling myself. I was not his wife, after all. I owe discretion to dear Aaron, and to the new Lord Galbreth, of course. And to you for that matter, my dear girl."

"You refine too much on my reputation," Marietta said. "It is not as though I came to you unblemished."

"Such a word! But you are too harsh with yourself. We know some knowledge of your . . . escapade has long since followed you here, but I have seen no evidence of anyone giving you the cut. If anyone refines too much, it is you, Marietta."

She declined to reply, instead taking her aunt's arm and leading her out of the house onto the path.

As they walked toward the church, Marietta reflected on the truth of her aunt's words. It was true that although rumor had followed her, for a brief time creating a ripple of abruptly interrupted conversations whenever Marietta had entered a room, the tattlemongers had long since given the matter up for juicier and fresher morsels. What had chased Marietta from London proper was little more than an anecdote here in rural Kendall Town.

Admittedly, however, the murmurs had not served to make her an eagerly sought partner at dances either. There were other girls to be flirted with, girls with monies, or with no scandal tainting their respectability.

Still, there was one fellow some people rather generously called her beau—but Marietta was not so sure "beau" was the correct word. Mr. Lemuel Walker's attentions were certainly recurrent, but for herself she would say they were no more than, well, lukewarm. He always had a dance with her when they met at the same functions—but just the one. He always made the opportunity to speak with her, or to sit next to her, but he never asked her to stroll alone in a garden with him. He came to call upon her and her aunt at their home, and only ever stayed for a very proper fifteen minutes. He spoke of the future as if they might share yet more time together, but he did not propose. Mr. Walker seemed to be . . . waiting, as if he were trying to decipher his feelings toward her.

And how did Marietta feel about *him*? He was certainly comely enough, even with skin made swarthy by time spent at sea. He stood with the straight-backed grace of a man of authority. He wore his hair longish, making the most of its smooth waves. His manners were impeccable, if a measure rigid, but perhaps that came from having once been in the military. There were few others, if any, who knew that Mr. Walker had not so long ago been *Captain* Walker, for he no longer wore his colors and he insisted upon the plainer salutation of "Mister." Marietta was perhaps the only local lady who knew that he had not merely resigned his commission, but had had it taken from him.

That was what they shared, of course: disgrace. Each had felt its sting. It was the very thing that had thrown them together, that had brought him to her side one night.

They had danced and enjoyed the sort of light banter such occasions demand, but when Mr. Walker had taken her back to her seat, he had sat down beside her.

"Do you know we have something in common, Miss Hampton?" he had asked, his features pleasantly arranged.

"Do we?" she had asked with some trepidation, for

the dismissal from her family home had been yet a
new wound to her, and each sideways glance or fan
raised to hide a whisper had stung her anew.

"Indeed. I have heard your history, you see."

She had begun to rise, but he had caught her hand
and kept her in her seat.

"Do not misunderstand me. I do not think you
wicked."

"Indeed not? How wondrous," she had replied,
looking for Aunt Silvia to come and rescue her, but
Aunt Silvia had had her back turned to her niece. As
salvation was not forthcoming, Marietta had chosen
to attack, by not permitting Mr. Walker to first an-
nounce her offense. "I question that you feel safe with
me here, Mr. Walker. Are you not afraid I shall produce a pistol and shoot you in the foot, as I do all
men?" The only way to defend herself was to make
light of the whispers and rumors.

He had grinned at her. "I understand your fiancé,
Mr. Sharr, was finally convinced that you did not wish
to marry him."

"It was the only way he would come to understand
that truth," Marietta had announced with a lifting of
her chin. "He was not sorely injured. And he was never
actually my fiancé."

"Word is that your parents thought he was."

"My parents neglected to inquire whether or not I
would accept his suit," she had replied haughtily, not
adding that she could no more have borne to marry
the wet-mouthed, fast-handed, posterior-pinching Mr.
Sharr than she could have wed a monkey from the
menagerie.

"Come, Miss Hampton, I am not here now to belittle your actions. I believe it took a certain courage to, er, dissuade your suitor as you did. I quite admire you."

Marietta had looked at him askance.

"Indeed, I wish to be your friend. To prove I mean what I say, let me tell you what no one else in this room has had the sense to discover."

He had gone on to reveal that while he was in the Royal Navy a superior had taken him in dislike and had set a series of incidents into play, the final result of which had been that Captain Walker had been forced to quietly surrender his commission or else face trumped up charges of far greater dishonor.

"What dishonor?" she had asked.

His upper lip had curled. "I will not speak of the foul lies he intended to foist upon me. Suffice it to say I had no witnesses—just as he had planned it—and could not defend myself. I chose the smaller indignity of retirement, for my family's sake."

"Then we are not so very alike, after all. I chose for myself, and not to please my family," she had said, lowering her gaze.

He had placed a finger under her chin, lifting her gaze to meet his once more. Shaking his head, he had smiled ever so slightly. "Never look down, my girl. When someone challenges your choice in this life— never back away."

Thinking of that moment now, she remembered how in that moment she had begun to realize Mr. Walker could be as charming as he could be forthright, had begun to see that perhaps he was right, perhaps they did indeed have something in common in having both had to create new lives for themselves.

"But," she said silently to herself now as she walked

arm-in-arm toward the church with her aunt. "But how do I *feel* about Mr. Walker?"

Very like him, she supposed on a sigh, for she too was waiting . . . waiting for that certain spark that indicated love, or at least attraction. Not the manner of spark she had felt looking at the new Lord Galbreth, whose very size and stature were such as to grasp a woman's notice, gifted as he was with the kind of masculine presence unlikely to be overlooked. No, surely Marietta sought some more noble flash of . . . what? Intuition? A kind of knowing that she and a certain someone would suit?

How did one decide to marry? Marietta could scarce look to Aunt Silvia for advice, for that lady had peculiar notions on the matter of marriage. Marietta supposed marriage was a simple enough decision if one had loving parents there to advise and direct—if one did not have a mama too mild to speak against her husband's dictates, and a papa too rigidly determined that his will would supersede all other desires.

Marietta usually tried to put memories of her papa's censure from her mind, but perhaps it was the somber mood of the day that brought them to the fore again. She knew she had never quite been the demure creature papa would have liked his only daughter to be. He had never raised his hand to her when he had found her breaking his prohibitions against climbing trees or wrestling in the dirt with her brothers—but the coldness of his stare when he had lectured her at every childhood infraction had been far worse than any blow. As she grew older, the lectures became colder, shorter, their very terseness making them terrible.

One summer Papa had sent Marietta to live with her mother's sister, Aunt Silvia. "Let her learn first-hand what it is to live in disgrace!" she remembered her father shouting at her mama. "Marietta shall soon see for herself the misfortunes that await a willful woman!"

She had not understood his words then, nor after she returned to the bosom of her family come autumn. While it was true that Aunt Silvia had not lived a well-monied existence, Marietta had found her aunt to be surprisingly content in her life, de-spite her separation from the various branches of her family tree. Silvia had her friends, her books from the lending library, and a variety of inexpensive hobbies, such as birdwatching, to occupy her days.

That summer had, in fact, been the first during which Marietta herself had been entirely happy, free to climb any tree or swing on any gate or walk along any fence top as she pleased, without fear of later ad-monitions. Aunt Silvia had not cared if twelve-year-old Marietta had come home after playing with muddy bare feet or a dusty hem, so long as Marietta did the washing up afterward, and sewed any rips caused by her exploring.

She had been too young to ask after the nature of Aunt Silvia's "disgrace," but had seen no evidence of it herself. Marietta's own disgraces always came from such things as not having clean enough hands, or from her ribbon having slipped crooked in her hair, or from trying to match her table manners to the rough and tumble ones of her brothers—and Aunt Silvia was clean and neat and had excellent manners, so Marietta could only be mystified at what her aunt could possibly have done to earn Papa's lasting disapproval.

When she had first returned to her parents' home, Marietta had determined that she would attempt to be the daughter her father wanted her to be. She had made sure her hair and hands and clothes were pristine on those occasions when the children were permitted to join the adults at the big dining room table. She had only tussled with her two younger brothers, Philip and Clarence, after Nurse thought they were all tucked abed for the night. She had never again hidden Papa's gunpowder, even though she could not bear his habit of shooting out the open den windows at whatever unfortunate creature dared to cross his garden or climb his fruit trees. She had bit her tongue a hundred, no, a thousand times, when she had been maligned for some wrongdoing.

It was only inevitable, Marietta later supposed, that she had begun to sorely miss the freedom she'd tasted that summer with Aunt Silvia . . . and when in the space of one week she had found herself banished for the third time to her room without supper, Marietta resolved that since she obviously could not please Papa, she would therefore only strive to please herself.

What had once been a quietly rocky relationship, became from that moment forward an openly contentious one. Marietta could not recall the next few years without wincing at the memory of things she had said to her papa, and things that had been said in return.

By some unspoken and mutual consent, by her seventeenth birthday she and her papa had developed an adeptness at avoiding too much of one another's company. A relative quiet had returned to the household, but it was a quiet that was thick with dissatisfaction and disapproval.

They had let it stand so for too long, Marietta saw that now. A keg of gunpowder is utterly silent as it awaits the flame that will light its fuse, but a terrible power waits within all the same. Three months ago, the careful veneer of familial tolerance Marietta and her father had playacted at for too long had suddenly slipped. A spark had been struck, and the explosion that had followed had blown Marietta's world apart. . . .

Marietta had warned her supposed suitor, Mr. Sharr, the day before that she would not be ill-used by him, that he was not free to press his kisses upon her, nor to feel the contours of her body at his will. Yet here was Mr. Sharr again today—no doubt feeling emboldened by the fact that Mama had meekly retreated and left the two of them alone together in Papa's den— daring to become all tentacles again.

"But, my love, we are promised to one another! It is for us to explore the extent of that promise as it pleases us," he had replied. "We need not be shy or reticent, now we are to be man and wife." He moistened his perpetually wet lips with his even wetter tongue and strained toward her.

Marietta slipped under his arm, evading his hold as well as his kiss. She moved rapidly across her father's den, being sure there stood a reading table as a barrier between herself and Mr. Sharr.

Within a week of his first call, she had come to the

conclusion that Mr. Sharr's attentions were less about love or even making a good alliance than they were about lust. He had a way of *looking* at her that made Marietta's stomach tighten with disquiet, and his touches had grown increasingly forward.

"I know my papa has accepted your suit, sir, but *I* have not," she told him stiffly, her dislike of him doubling with every word he uttered, every impropriety he exercised.

"Come along then, my girl! Why hesitate a moment longer? Say you'll have me." He stepped back, allowing her a full view of his length, as though the sight of his sartorial splendor alone would eliminate any doubts she might harbor. While it was true that Mr. Sharr knew how to dress complete to a shade, all the finery in the world could not make up for his insipid conversation, his infrequent and patently insincere laugh and, most of all, his grasping hands. Whatever could her papa have been thinking to even allow this coxcomb in the house, let alone to accept Mr. Sharr's suit on her behalf? The answer to that was simple enough to arrive at: Papa had been thinking of removing his perpetually troublesome daughter from his home, and so had accepted the very first offer to come his way.

"I tell you now, Mr. Sharr, as plainly as I may, that I do not accept you, nor will I ever. I thank you for the honor you have done me," Marietta said through tight lips, "but now I really must bid good day to you." She turned her back to him to indicate she had no more to say on the matter, her hands gripping the edge of her father's desk to keep them from reaching up to brush away the feel of where his hands had touched her arms.

"Such missishness, my dear!" he exclaimed, crossing to place his hands on her shoulders. "Come, you have but to say yes and then we will sup of the fruits of love. Just a bit, my girl, I assure you. Just enough to be sure we suit. You need not be so afraid. Let me show you what joy awaits you once we are married." His hands began to slide down and forward, as though to cup her breasts.

She stared at the desktop, beginning to quiver with outrage and loathing, when her gaze fixed on the special stand on which her father kept his brace of pistols mounted. She knew the weapons would be primed and readied to be fired; she could smell the faint odor of the gunpowder, sitting in the pan on each pistol, awaiting the hammer's strike.

Marietta scarcely thought, her hand moving as though on its own to reach for the nearest pistol, pulling it from the stand. She spun to face Mr. Sharr, the barrel of the pistol raised to point at his left eye. "I am most sincere in what I say, Mr. Sharr," she said firmly, coolly.

He took a startled step away, his hands dropping to his sides. He scowled. "Why, you little devil cat! I begin to rethink this proposition of marriage myself, if this is your manner! I suppose you are hoping for a title, as if my thirty thousand a year is not the very best offer you could ever hope to have made to you." He stuck his thumbs in his waistcoat pockets, and sniffed. "You overrate your charms, baggage."

"I am perfectly content for you to think me lacking in charms, so long as you leave me be and no longer think to press your suit or your attentions on me," Marietta said, belatedly remembering to grasp the dogshead hammer with her two thumbs and cock it back.

Mr. Sharr frowned even more deeply, but then slowly his brow cleared, and an unpleasant little smile replaced the scowl. "By gad, your temper needs trimming, my girl! And I think I am just the one to do it, too."

He stepped toward her again, pressing Marietta against the desk's edge, his hand closing around the wrist of the hand in which she held the gun. He pushed the barrel downward, and laughingly said, "Who leaves a pistol primed and readied, my girl?" He shook his head, making a tsking sound with his tongue. "No one. It is very bad for the weapon to be left so, of course."

She did not attempt to try and pull her hand up, knowing he could easily overpower her. Instead she looked down at the weapon, wondering if she could have actually used it against him anyway . . . and saw that the barrel aimed directly at Mr. Sharr's foot. Her finger moved to the trigger, but she exerted no pressure on the metal.

Why should she harm him? She could not be *forced* to marry Mr. Sharr. No clergyman would perform a marriage wherein the bride would clearly be so unwilling as Marietta would be seen to be. Papa would not stoop to bribery, nor to getting the clergyman so drunk the man did not know better.

Her papa could—and no doubt would—lecture her. He could lock her in her room, forbid her food, forbid the servants to supply wood for a fire on her grate—he could do a hundred unhappy things in an attempt to persuade Marietta to accept Mr. Sharr's suit—but he could not *make* her do it. Sixty years ago it might have been possible to force a marriage, but Marietta knew the law, that it was impossible for anyone to force another into a bonding to which he or she did not consent.

Of course, Marietta added in a mental note that made her stomach roil with nausea, there was little that protected her from Mr. Sharr's forward attentions so long as Papa saw fit to allow them to continue. The idea of days, or even weeks, of Mr. Sharr coming to call, of his grasping hands, one of which even now snaked around her waist and pulled her closer, sent a shiver of disgust down her spine.

Mr. Sharr's wet lips pressed against Marietta's cheek, and she jerked her head down and to one side—the side still holding the pistol, still pointed at his foot.

"Please stop," she said, trying to press away from his chest with the one hand that did not hold the pistol.

Mr. Sharr pulled her closer yet, pressing his open mouth against the flesh of her forehead where it met the line of her hair. "You are a delicious little baggage, you are, my dear," he murmured near her ear.

"Stop it!" she said again, her voice growing shrill as she tried to wriggle away. "Papa!" she cried out. Her papa might want her to wed, might even believe he did his daughter a favor to encourage this man with thirty thousand pounds a year—but even Papa would not bear this manner of assault on her person.

But why did a servant not come? Why did the door

to the den remain so firmly closed, despite the fact
she called out?

Marietta felt Mr. Sharr's tongue, long and wet, as
he kissed her temple. She made an inarticulate protest, a fierce noise that seemed to sharply focus her
comprehension of what must be happening: her papa
must be too trusting, must have warned or shooed any
servant from the area, knowing as he did that Marietta
had already protested several times that she did not
wish to see Mr. Sharr anymore, that she would seek
their help to avoid being alone in Mr. Sharr's company
wherein he could again press his suit. . . . If she
screamed, would anyone come? And even if he came,
would Papa believe the nature of these improprieties
as Marietta told them to him?

She pictured days . . . weeks, of missed meals, of a
cold room, of Mr. Sharr calling again, of repeating
this assault, of the liberties becoming more and more
brazen. . . . Marietta's head swam. She shuddered,
and then she screamed as there came a bright flash.
It was immediately followed by a thunderous roar, and
almost as quickly a shout of pain from Mr. Sharr.

Marietta blinked and focused her gaze, seeing the
gaping hole in Mr. Sharr's Hessian boot, somewhere
in the vicinity of his little toe. She gave a very tiny
shriek of astonishment to know that she had accidentally squeezed the trigger.

"You—! You *fiend!*" Mr. Sharr gasped. He released
her and began to hop on his uninjured foot, gasping
in pain once more before going on to call her a number of names, some of whose meaning she could only
guess at.

He was still swearing when the first servant arrived

to stare at the scene, the footman's gape-mouthed shock striking Marietta as a weirdly humorous counterpoint to Mr. Sharr's livid rage.

Despite Mr. Sharr's vitriolic tirade, Marietta felt a grin tugging at her lips. It seemed to her that Mr. Sharr would be most unlikely to renew his suit. Her grin, no doubt, had more to do with shock than relief, but relief flooded her all the same.

That is, until she saw the look on Papa's face when he entered the room, his dark scowl shattering any faint overlay of humor in the situation.

It was the total denial of compassion, the severity of his judgment as to what she had done, that ever after remained uppermost in Marietta's recollection of the whole miserable circumstance that her entire family went on to label "Marietta's disgrace."

Thinking of it now as she and Aunt Silvia made their way to the funeral, Marietta grimaced yet again at the thought of the days that followed directly after the shooting.

It could have been worse, admittedly. The fact the man lost a toe was an unfortunate enough thing, but Marietta shuddered to think how easily things could have gone much further amiss: what if she had accidentally killed Mr. Sharr?

The shooting could not be smoothed over, try as Papa might. Mr. Sharr was too wealthy a man to accept money from Marietta's family to remain silent—he had made it clear he meant to be anything but close-mouthed over the affair. The tale had spread throughout London in less than a day.

Truly, what were Marietta's parents to do? The only real alternative to banishing their daughter was to banish the entire family from London—and that would not have been fair to Marietta's brothers. No, the most expedient solution had been to send Marietta off to the country in disgrace.

Her lips thinned for one brief moment into a bitter line. Although there had been a certain measure of logic behind the punishment—banishment from Society—that Papa had seen fit to mete out, it had been unnecessarily harsh that she was to have nothing more than the most meager of incomes to accompany her.

"This banishment is not absolute," her father had told her in his sternest, coldest voice, a voice that scarce allowed her to hope for any kind of reprieve. "But there is only one way you have of ever being again in this family's good graces: that is for you to marry. Do not think to darken my door ever again, not unless there is a husband at your side. You must understand completely that I am done coping with your stubborn nature. That duty must fall on another."

And not just any marriage would do, Papa went on to explain—Marietta would have to somehow magically win the regard of another gentleman with pockets as plump as Mr. Sharr's—or perhaps a title of baron or better would serve as well.

Never mind that Papa had seen to it that the possibility of such an occurrence was utterly unattainable—for why would such a nonpareil marry a mere knight's disgraced, disavowed and all-but-penniless daughter?

Marietta had not bothered to respond that even should she one day take a husband, why would she ever care to bring him to a home so filled with unwelcome for her presence?

A murmur of distant voices interrupted the dark memories, and Marietta shook her head, to clear it of thoughts as grey and depressing as the clouds above. She looked up to see that she and Aunt Silvia had nearly come to the church. A steady throng of mourners had responded to the passing bells, and were slowly filing past the church's opened doors to find their seats for the service.

"Miss Nicholson," called one of Aunt Silvia's acquaintances, Mrs. Pepperidge, who lifted her folded black fan in greeting. Marietta surrendered her aunt's arm to that of her friend, glad for any distraction that might serve to stem Aunt Silvia's weeping. As it was, Silvia's chin trembled for a moment before she managed to return her friend's greeting, but perhaps Mrs. Pepperidge's usual prattle would serve to give Aunt Silvia something to concentrate on rather than the sad ceremony soon to begin.

A flash of movement in the trees edging one side of the churchyard caught Marietta's eye. She looked to see which of her neighbors came that way, and was surprised to spy Lord Galbreth's large form strolling beneath the shading trees. She began to turn away, but at that moment he glanced up and their gazes met across the way. He nodded and reached to politely tip his hat. Marietta waited for him to reach her side, which he achieved in only a dozen long strides.

Instead of falling into step together as she expected, Lord Galbreth came to a halt at her side. He glanced toward the church, but then fixed his attention on her. "Miss Hampton," he said over a sketched bow.

"Lord Galbreth," she returned with a curtsy. "My condolences, sir, on this sad day."

He nodded. "Thank you." He fell silent, then glanced around, and finally back at Marietta. It seemed to her that his expression was rather sheepish, where she would have more expected a grim tolerance for the duty awaiting him.

He gestured toward the trees, then back toward the church. "I was walking . . . delaying going within, as you could perhaps have guessed."

She lifted her eyebrows in mild surprise at the forthright comment.

"I am aware I ought to have been standing in the doorway, shaking hands and accepting everyone's condolences, but . ." His words trailed away.

"An observance such as this is naturally a burden," she murmured, knowing something of the sting of loss he must be feeling no matter how little he had known his father. She had ached with a similar pain, for it was very like a death to have been banished from her family, no matter the disharmony in the household.

The sheepish look deepened. "Miss Hampton, I believe I have misled you. I have implied I am awash in grief. While that may be true, to one degree or another—" He hesitated, and actually blushed.

"My lord?"

His lips parted, but then he hesitated again, only to blurt out, "You will think me the greatest nodcock, but the truth is only this morning did it occur to me that I have nothing at all to wear that is black, not even my hat." He touched a finger to his rich brown top hat fashionably made of beaver pelt, and blushed again. "Once I decided I would set sail for England, I gave away everything I owned that was black. I hope you do not think me unfeeling. Although my mother had but recently passed away, I meant no disrespect to her memory, but . . . I was preparing to travel. And I wished to be done with death. . . . I had no thought of being so soon again in mourning."

It occurred to Marietta that he could well have come to this country thinking he had but one immediate relative left: his father. Aunt Silvia had told her that his mother was gone, and Marietta had heard not one word to indicate that the new Lord Galbreth had any siblings. He wore no wedding ring, nor had he spoken of needing to return to a wife or sweetheart in America; it would seem he was a man utterly devoid of any close kin. He could hardly be expected to don a show of deep mourning for some cousin or other he had never met, and so his actions were perfectly understandable.

"The thing of it is . . . can you tell me, Miss Hampton, will I dishonor my father by this lack? This dark blue was the best I could manage on such short notice. Ought I to see if perhaps the rector has a coat I might borrow? And, while I am asking questions, was it proper that I invited the servants to the funeral? That only seemed in keeping, with their having served him so long. But is it done here in England?"

Marietta kept a soft smile of sympathy from forming on her lips, for the poor man could well take it amiss and be offended by it. He was obviously unsettled. It had not occurred to her before that the usual burden of dealing with a death might be worsened by an unfamiliarity with the customs of the land in which the deceased was to be buried.

"As to your second concern, it is certainly acceptable that the servants should attend the rites for your father, just as I gather it is in America," she assured him, watching relief spread over his features. "As to the other, yes, it is peculiar that you have no black to wear. You will have to have some items made up for you, I am afraid, to use for the next six months of mourning."

"Six months?" His relief visibly increased. "Just as is the custom in America."

"We English are cousins to the Americans, you will recall." Now Marietta did allow the smile to form. "Some would say your parent."

" 'We' indeed. I know my accent owes more to Kentucky than Kent, but do not forget I am an Englishman born."

She acknowledged that with a nod. "I admit there is something decidedly 'American' about you that leads me to forget you were not born there." She lowered her gaze from his, for somehow her words had carried a resonance that seemed more particular than she had intended them to be, and the questioning gaze he returned seemed to take note of that fact.

"But I suspect the two countries share many customs," she hurried on, adding a quick smile. "However, time grows short in which I can help you with the moment's immediate concern." She glanced about, to be sure no one was watching.

"What are you doing?" he asked as she removed her bonnet.

She tore one of the long crepe ribbons that trailed

from the black-painted straw crown, and shook her head to stop his protest.

"I shall scarce miss it," she said. She placed her bonnet once again atop her head, then reached to tie the ribbon around the sleeve of his coat. Even though the brush of her fingers was light, her touch revealed there was nothing soft about the thick expanse of muscles that was his upper arm. She stepped back, glad to think that perhaps her black gloves hid any trembling sign of the sudden and curious tingling that had sprung to life in her fingertips. "There!" she said, perhaps a trifle too brightly. "It is not all you could wish for the day, but it will serve well enough."

He glanced down at the black bow, and then met her gaze once more with his own. "Thank you," he said, his voice quietly sincere.

"You are very welcome," she murmured, turning her eyes down and away from his blue-eyed gaze.

He offered her his arm, and escorted her to the door of the church, but there she stepped back. "You must go ahead."

"Ladies first—"

It was her turn to blush. She wished her cheeks had not heated so, for what would the few stragglers who now hurried toward the church think of such color in her face? "It might appear . . . peculiar, my lord, if I were to come in on your arm."

He frowned for a moment, but then his brow cleared, and she suspected he understood the awkwardness of such seeming familiarity among strangers—one of whom lived in the dower house on the other's estate. "Of course," he said simply, just before he sketched her a quick bow, doffed his hat, and turned to enter the church.

Marietta waited a full minute, allowing the local baker and his wife to make an entry before she executed her own. As she found her seat next to Aunt Silvia in the general pews behind the family boxes, she thought to herself *now here is yet another dilemma!* Whereas the chaperonage she and Aunt Silvia granted one another had always seemed sufficient before, was it enough now? It was one thing to live on the estate of an older gentleman well known to the locals—but another altogether for the two unmarried ladies to be living so near the young and unknown stranger who had arrived among them. Everything about the new Lord Galbreth would be suspect to the villagers—including the fact that two women lacking any male protection were residing in his dower house.

Marietta tried not to squirm in her seat, and to keep her features calmly arranged, well aware that if she had thought to question the situation, so would others. She must present the very attitude of indifference, at least in all matters relating to the new Lord Galbreth. There were problems enough to overcome; she did not need the added burden of local gossip and speculation.

She glanced out of the corner of her eye toward Lord Galbreth, and saw her ribbon tied about his sleeve. Hopefully no one would notice it was of the right length and fabric to have come from her bonnet. Although, she tried to assure herself, even if they did, the most vicious tattlemonger could make little enough sport of such a simple favor, surely?

She sighed and shook her head once, and tried

to concentrate on the rector's words of heavenly love and rewards. The words jumbled quickly, though, for her attention was caught by the sight of Lord Galbreth's head and shoulders where they rose above the box of his family pew. An errant beam of sunlight had found its way past the gloomy clouds, shining through the colored stained glass situated high above him in the church wall. The light shone down on Lord Galbreth, marking his face and clothes with a patchwork of colors.

Something tugged deep inside Marietta. Call it a pang of sympathy for that sun-touched soul sitting there, all alone in his box, utterly bereft of family, without even a single friend by his side. She had wished him back to America, but for selfish reasons, in the desperate hope that his going would allow the little world she had built for herself to remain as it had been. But now she wished him back for his sake, back to the friends, mentors, confidantes he surely possessed there.

"You appear quite pale of a sudden, Marietta," Aunt Silvia whispered near her ear. "Are you ailing?"

"No, I—it is just . . . only look at Lord Galbreth, Aunt Silvia! I wish we might join him in his box, or ask him to join us. It is too sad, him sitting there all alone."

"It is as well we cannot, for I should burst into noisy tears either way," Aunt Silvia whispered in an unusually subdued tone that reflected her tendency to do just that. "He has much the look of Aaron about him, which I can bear at a distance, but . . ." Her words trailed away.

Marietta reached to pat her aunt's hand.

Silvia dabbed at her eyes with a kerchief. "I must say it is very good of you to wish to console him, my dear. You are a true Christian, to wish to comfort your enemy."

Marietta blinked at the word, although she might have used it herself only a day earlier. But perhaps it was entirely apt. Perhaps he would prove himself to be an ogre, and a tyrant, and a destroyer of all Marietta's exertions to better her lot—she had met him but thrice, and only this last encounter long enough to judge something of his nature.

Was she a fool to feel sorry for the man, based only on ten minutes' conversation? What did she really know of him, other than that in the unhappy circumstance of his father's funeral, he had for a moment lost his poise? Was a loss of poise necessarily a measure of kindness, or reasonableness? Surely it was unwise to lower her caution, to allow her thinking to cloud with sympathy, a sympathy unwarranted by any real knowledge of Lord Galbreth's temperament or attributes. Today he thanked her for her ribbon; tomorrow he could cast her from her home.

Marietta looked away from where the light gilded Lord Galbreth's brown hair, deliberately concentrating her attention on Aunt Silvia, whose calm demeanor was slowly seeping away under a flow of silently surrendered tears. Marietta only hoped that after today there would be no additional reason to weep, no insistence that she and her aunt must live elsewhere, must try to find a new place, a new way in which to go on.

She had learned to survive, to use her wits. She would not now lose them to a smile and a sunbeam.

Seven

Halfway through the church service, a disturbance at the church's entry caused Fane to twist his head and look to see who had belatedly arrived. His glance showed him white breeches and hose, over which resided a dark blue military coat complete with gold frogging over white lapels and cuffs, and a gold-trimmed hat tucked under the man's arm. Fane felt himself blanch.

It was only a moment more before he realized the white-haired gentleman who now took a seat on the nearest bench was far too old to be Captain Walker, as Fane had for a moment feared him to be. Even should his hair have turned utterly white in the ensuing year since Fane had last seen Walker, he could not have shrunk four or five inches to equal this man's height. And what could possibly bring the haughty Captain Walker to bucolic Kendall Town anyway? No, a man like Walker would live in London, and would retire after the Season to Brighton or Bath or some other crowded civic setting where his . . . *appetites* could be satisfied. The older man who had belatedly entered was just some officer with local connections, no doubt dressed in his naval finery in honor of the funeral service.

Captain Walker. Fane had pondered that name even as he had hesitated a moment before laying down the money to buy his passage to England.

He did not know Captain Walker's fate; he only knew the war between England and America that had begun in 1812 was now ended, and that men like Captain Walker who had once sailed off the eastern coast of America could no longer harass and unlawfully hold the citizens of Fane's borrowed homeland. They could not now—but not so long ago, under British law, the act of impressing British-born "Americans" into the Royal Navy had been perfectly legal. In fact, impressment was still legal, even if the ending of the war meant the capture of any American, British-born or not, was officially no longer tolerated.

"Captain Walker," Fane repeated the name aloud, under his breath, and shook his head at the memories the name invoked. It conjured pictures of smug superiority, of unearned harshness . . . and a shrouded secret. A two-sided secret shared between the two men, each of whom could condemn the other.

Fane's share in the secret had not mattered until he set foot aboard a vessel bound for England, for so long as he lived in America it would be his secret to keep. However, the minute he had placed his person on a British ship, had placed himself within the confines of British authority, the secret had mattered very much.

He had used the name Fane Westby when he had registered for the journey—not the "Peter White" he had grown up believing his name to be. It was the first time he had called himself by this new name, for he had deliberately chosen to leave his American neighbors with no knowledge of any "Fane Westby." Should he stay in England, he must not have Peter White's debacle follow him. Should he return to America, he would want to return to the life he had known there, to the name he was known by. Captain Walker and the British Navy knew the name Peter White; the name was marked in their infernal records as "Deserter."

That knowledge had been Fane's one hesitation in deciding to come to meet his father. There were perhaps a half-dozen British seamen who could put the name of Peter White with the face of Fane Westby, and Captain Walker was one of them. The others may have long since forgotten him—he had been, after all, only one American among many whose ship they had confiscated and whom they had pressed into service. But Captain Walker had every reason to remember his face, and to curse it.

Fane shook his head to clear it of thoughts almost as dismal as the funereal music now playing. The movement caused the black bow on his sleeve to tremble, and Fane felt his attention shift to the lady who had tied it there. He indirectly peered at Miss Hampton from the corners of his eyes, thinking her assistance had been a welcome buoy in the sea of uncertainty in which he had found himself. She could have laughed at his ignorance, could have looked askance at the impulse that had resulted in his being incorrectly attired. Instead she had only gently teased him a little, and had damaged her own bonnet for his benefit. Hardly what one would expect from a strumpet. . . .

He shook his head, denying to himself that Miss Hampton could be any true sort of doxie. He knew almost nothing of her, but he knew "strumpet" was already a word he would not apply to her again. Her banishment into living with her aunt had surely been caused by some form of misguidance or misfortune, but he was willing to wager it was not because Miss Hampton was a lightskirt. Peculiar that he should feel so certain of the fact, on so short an acquaintance (and especially given that her aunt had chosen to be a man's mistress), but there it was.

Curious. And even more curious that he felt a growing satisfaction with his decision to decipher the puzzle of the ladies in the dower house, to seeing that this small mystery was solved before he made his own decision as to whether or not he would return to America.

The rector stuttered just then, and Fane realized that in his preoccupation with his own thoughts, his expression had surely shifted from one of satisfaction to a scowl. Fane made an effort to rearrange his features into a neutral expression, and it was not until the rector had resumed a smoother oratory that Fane turned his thoughts again to what had caused him to scowl in the first place: if he *did* return to America, what exactly did he have to return *to*?

There was his position, importer for the largest coffee-house in the heart of Philadelphia. There were his friends, Martin, Geoffrey, Willie—all good fellows known since childhood.

Too, there was a single, cold stone in a graveyard.

So what do I have here? a cynical voice in his head replied. *A stone in a graveyard. And a church box in which I sit all by myself.*

There really was no dilemma. Of course he would

return to America. What kind of future could a deserter from the Royal Navy hope to find in England anyway, even should he wish to pursue one here?

"How pleased we are to meet you, my lord," simpered a short, broad woman whose name Fane could not recall five seconds after the introductions had been made. But then again the gathering of mourners at Westby Hall after the funeral services had made for an afternoon filled with unfamiliar names and faces.

There was only one face Fane was relieved to find nowhere among the callers: Captain Walker. It was evidently even as Fane had supposed it to be: Walker was not a man to wile away his hours in some bucolic hamlet.

"May I say what a delight it was for us to hear that Lord Galbreth's son had returned," the woman went on.

"Yes, thank you," Fane murmured.

"And of course it is so pleasant to have a young man once again inhabiting Westby Hall," the woman continued. She glanced at her daughter, a glum-faced and silent little creature whose name had also escaped Fane.

The mother then cocked her head coyly to one side. "But, do you know, no one can tell me if we are soon to have the pleasure of meeting your lady when she comes from America. Or are you perhaps not yet married, my lord?"

"No," Fane said shortly, for he had felt the speculative glances on him these two hours past. Though, there was a side of him that had to admire the woman for asking the question that a dozen other curious mamas with marriageable daughters had not quite dared to voice on this day of burial.

The woman brightened visibly and turned once more to her daughter. "Not married! Did you hear, Lula?" Before she could lure her shy daughter back into the conversation, however, Fane bowed and excused himself, mumbling something vague about needing to attend to some matter.

He retreated to an alcove, moving to where he could be half-hidden by the draping curtain, in the dim hope that he might have a few moments to himself. A quick glance left him reasonably assured his retreat had not been noted. It would not be long, however, before his absence was remarked upon, for he had no doubt he was the principle subject of the day's conversation. It seemed no one in the district was the slightest bit reticent about wishing to view the "prodigal son" for themselves—under the guise of coming to offer their condolences, of course.

Although, Fane amended, the condolences had long since given way to questions—rude questions at that. His father was scarcely covered over with dirt, and yet here were all the local gentry, assessing the new lord's worth and availability, asking not-so-subtle questions about income and availability that would have put a blush to the lowest rustic back home in Philadelphia. Home indeed! Fane scowled as he gazed out the alcove window at the foreign sight of English sheep grazing on English fields, and thought that this company was enough to make even the staunchest man think of fleeing England.

Fleeing?

An interesting choice of word, Fane thought with a frown. But it was the proper one, for it would indeed be no more than an ignominious retreat should he allow such fawning, scraping creatures to chase him away before he was ready to leave. The thought left a bad taste in his mouth.

"Galbreth, my dear host! Best of all hosts, I assure you," said a young fop named Mr. Damson who pushed the curtain aside. A scent of wine came with him, revealing Mr. Damson had made free with the champagne or the sherry that had been served to the guests.

Fane gathered himself, stepping out from the alcove to nod at Mr. Damson, who was attended by a few other young bucks. The fellow had been introduced by one Lord Roderick, who had presumed an acquaintance from the fact that he had himself been introduced only a few minutes earlier.

"The lads and I have been pondering the question," Mr. Damson went on, seemingly oblivious to the fact that Fane had not responded, "on whether or not you mean to keep your house in London?"

Fane returned a blank expression. "I have not decided," he replied evenly; he had made no decision because he'd had no notion there was a London home to inherit.

"It is very near Almack's, if you should not happen to know," Mr. Damson said with a slow smile that hinted even more at inebriation. He crossed one foot over the other, leaned against the nearby wall, and swung an eyeglass back and forth from where its ribbon wrapped around his finger. "I had the privilege of calling at Almack's, I did," Mr. Damson went on, his voice mildly slurred. "You do know what Almack's is, do you not, Galbreth? But of course you must! Everyone knows 'bout Almack's. Do you hope to subscribe, Lord Galbreth?"

"I could not say."

Mr. Damson smirked, and Sir Roderick with him. One of the young bucks chortled.

"Too true! Too true, Lord Galbreth. 'Tis, after all, not ours to say who shall attend and who shall not, is it?" Mr. Damson said, his amusement evident. "We must wait upon the whim of one of the all-powerful patronesses to allow us entry. We must be esteemed by one of the good ladies as being *appropriate* company."

There was a keen amusement in Mr. Damson's eyes that caused Fane to stiffen. Although he had an idea that Almack's was some manner of London club wherein both sexes partook of dancing, that was all he knew of the place. From what Mr. Damson said, it would seem it was an exclusive realm . . . and from the man's bright-eyed, eager gawking—not to mention that of the surrounding dozen or more listeners—it seemed clear the man had decided to make Fane the butt of some manner of japery. It was not difficult to surmise that Mr. Damson and his friends found the new Lord Galbreth wanting, that they thought it highly unlikely that Fane would be welcome at this exclusive place known as Almack's.

"And who do the patronesses of this Almack's consider *appropriate* company, Mr. Damson?" he said coolly. "I should suppose they might look for those who can keep a civil tongue in their head—but perhaps you would not know for a certainty, having only been allowed within once yourself."

Now it was Mr. Damson's turn to stiffen his stance. "Well, for one, they do not allow *Americans,* sirrah," Damson said on a superior sniff.

"Come, come," said a female voice. "That is not true at all, Mr. Damson."

The crowd, like so many crows all in their black plumage, parted to reveal Miss Hampton as she swept toward Fane. She was of course dressed equally in black, as the ceremony had dictated, and the color seemed to lend to her frowning countenance something of what one might expect to see were she a reproving angel.

"I have myself met any number of Americans at Almack's," she told Mr. Damson, and the look in her eyes as she went on to survey the gathered crowd was a challenge, as if she dared anyone who might know of it to mention her banishment from London. No one rose to the challenge, however, and she went on. "Even were Americans never welcome at Almack's, Mr. Damson, that would bear no meaning for Lord Galbreth. You seem to have forgot that he is himself an Englishman born."

Mr. Damson's cheeks, already warmed by wine, now flushed an even rosier hue in silent acknowledgment of his lapse. " 'Tis his uncivilized accent that quite threw me off—"

Miss Hampton turned her back to him, the motion effectively cutting off his protest, and she stepped forward to Fane's side. "Have you met everyone, my lord? Excellent!" she said without waiting for his reply. "Then it only behooves us, your guests, to extend our farewells, that you might know some peace and privacy on this unhappy day."

The assembled throng grumbled under their collective breaths and shuffled their shoes on the floor tiles, but there was no way to graciously refute Miss Hampton's pronouncement. Fane found that a queue of guests sprang into instant life. One by one, the mourners offered their farewells before moving to retrieve their hats and cloaks and reticules, which Poole and the small army of footmen who had previously been serving sherry and cake now handed out.

When perhaps half the people were already gone, it was Miss Hampton and her aunt's turn to make their farewells and murmur words of comfort to him over their curtsies.

"Thank you," he said with emphasis to Miss Hampton, leaning toward her in the guise of a bow to quickly add in a low voice, "for saving me from Damson's boorishness."

"I cannot bear a bully," she whispered in return. She stepped back and nodded briefly, but not before Fane had noted the serious undertone in her words. Had someone bullied Miss Hampton once upon a time? Fane considered her for a long moment; if this woman was indeed a doxie, then she was of the "golden-hearted" variety, always ready with a kind word or action to soothe over an awkward moment. Yet she returned his gaze with the same boldness she had demonstrated when first they'd met, when he was locked out of the gate and she sat self-importantly atop the horse whose mane she had plaited with flowers. Hers was a knowing gaze, aged beyond the youth of her features, a seasoned gaze that seemed to argue a lack of innocence . . . but, then again, the memory of those plaited flowers seemed to argue the other way.

She was a true enigma, he told himself with an interior shake of the head, belatedly turning to the woman's aunt.

As he looked down at her, Miss Nicholson's eyes filled with tears, and he recalled that this woman's loss in some ways exceeded his own. Perhaps he ought to feel resentment that the mistress who had taken his mother's place had the gall to attend his father's funeral—but then again it would have looked even stranger if she had not, since she lived on the estate. Truth be told, Fane could summon no resentment for the woman.

"It was good of you to come, Miss Nicholson," he said, and took up her hand to place an airy kiss above her fingers.

She nodded. He suspected she could not speak for the tears that blocked her throat.

"But this is only too perfect a moment to ask you a question that I have been pondering," said the next woman in line—a Mrs. Leffler, he recalled. She spoke as if to Fane, but it was to Miss Hampton that Mrs. Leffler looked.

"Question?" Fane echoed.

"Of these two ladies, of course! My dear Miss Nicholson, Miss Hampton, I have been trying to suppose where you mean to make your home now," Mrs. Leffler asked with a smile that could not quite hide the keen edge in her inquiry.

"Make our home?" Miss Hampton repeated as Fane watched the color drain from her face.

"Why, it is obvious you cannot remain in the estate's

dower house, of course," Mrs. Leffler asserted. She nodded at Fane. "No insult intended toward yourself, my lord, but of course it is not the thing at all to have them there."

Fane felt the muscles of his back tense, as much at Miss Hampton's unexpected loss of color as at Mrs. Leffler's tone, which seemed to him to be deceitfully affable. "Why ever not?" he asked.

Miss Hampton threw him a startled glance.

"Well, surely it is obvious why not, my lord. The ladies cannot remain in the house as they have, not with you, a bachelor, so near at hand—"

"But my father was all but a bachelor, in truth if not in law," Fane stated, keeping his expression blank, as if he could not comprehend the woman's protest.

"But your father was a married man. You, my lord, are not. We must think of the proprieties," Mrs. Leffler huffed.

Fane struggled to keep a growing irritation at bay, for he knew it was the way of the world for people to share their opinions, whether the listener wished to hear them or not. Especially if the one receiving the opinions was an outsider come into a small and close community.

"But I thought I understood that here in England you have tenants, much the way we do in America." He frowned, as if an idea had just occurred to him. "Or can you be . . ." he let his words trail away for a moment, as if he were trying to grasp a totally alien thought. "Can you be saying you believe my conduct may not be above reproach?"

"Well, of course I do not mean to imply that, my

lord," Mrs. Leffler said in a fluster, twin spots of color blooming on her cheeks.

He allowed his features to clear. "No, of course not," he said, adding a smile.

One side of Mrs. Leffler's mouth turned up in a feeble echo of his smile, and she quickly murmured her goodbyes. However, as she walked away, she threw a speaking backward glance at Miss Hampton.

Fane took a step forward, intending to murmur some dismissive remark regarding the lady's claims of impropriety, but Miss Hampton turned away abruptly, pulling her aunt along with her.

So the damage begins, Fane thought to himself with a strange sinking sensation. A declaration of unseemliness had been made, no matter that Fane had tried to negate it. So much for setting things aright before he left! Miss Nicholson and her niece would, invariably, become the subject of speculation and gossip . . . as would he, if he took no action to correct the situation.

It seemed he must ask the ladies to move out.

His very proximity to their home threatened their reputations. It was one thing for the elder lady to live in the dower house, but, even with her chaperonage, Fane had to admit that the dower house's isolated nearness to his home was a threat to Miss Hampton. And according to Bintliff, Miss Hampton possessed good standing in this village; whatever her sin, she had not visited its like upon these people. Far be it from him to harm that standing—after all, she was nearly as much an outsider to these country folk as he was himself. He would not cast the first stone.

The difficulty lay in the simple fact that she was

young, as was he, and she was comely to look upon. How could anyone help but speculate as to an illicit union between them? Only look to his own reaction—an uncomfortable shifting of his shoulders beneath his fitted coat as he momentarily imagined holding Miss Hampton in his arms—to see the situation was ripe for conjecture.

Too, how well had the aunt's arrangement with Fane's papa been kept a secret? Was Miss Nicholson's behavior already whispered about behind closed doors? Was she truly in any kind of position to meaningfully play the duenna to her niece? To judge by Mrs. Leffler's quick questioning of the situation, it seemed perhaps not.

Well, obviously Fane must see to it that the ladies found a new home. But what if Father's will granted the use of the dower house to them? They would have to be paid from the estate, to compensate them for moving elsewhere. Clearly this move would be a difficult situation, at best, for how could Fane be seen to provide them with any funds? That would hardly serve the purpose of saving their reputations!

It was a conundrum.

Fane smiled ever so slightly to himself. In all his years of sailing to far climes, trading for coffee beans with natives, and glimpsing exotic customs, never before in one day's time had he encountered both an enigma and a conundrum. The question was, was it England itself that presented these mystifications . . . or a certain English miss?

Eight

Fane's favorite time of day had always been dusk, when magic danced in the dim grey light that existed between day and night, when reveries could be soft-edged and yielding, and hopes seemed poignant yet possible. But dusk was not a time for deep and clear-minded thought, which Fane knew he must bring himself to eventually. For now, after the last of the funeral guests left in the dimness of late near-evening, he fell to his bed and chose dreams over contemplation.

He rose before dawn, however, awakened by the instinct to sort his thoughts in the crisp, cool air that preceded the sunlight. He dressed, and donned his caped greatcoat and his curly-brimmed hat. He left the house without encountering anyone, not even the butler Poole, who was no doubt warming his hands before the fire in the kitchens, along with those maids who would soon be starting new fires on some grates and sweeping out the ashes from others.

Fane walked along the confines of his father's estate, knowing the fence at the far rear of the property was not the end of the Galbreth land belonging with the house, but more likely just a barrier to keep wandering cattle from consuming the budding gardens that surrounded the house. This, all this presumably, was his, should he wish to reach out and accept it.

He came to the crest of a low hill, and thoughtfully gazed out upon the surrounding land. There was land aplenty in America—but none of it belonged to him, not even the rental property he had shared with Mama. In his absence, a solicitor paid the owner, Mr. Garvey, the monthly rent for the privilege of having a place for Fane to call home.

No, Fane had owned no land, nor the ships on which he had spent half his adult years. In the dark before dawn, it was easy to compare the low rolling hills of countryside around him as resembling the slowly undulating waves of a peaceful sea. But it was no surging deck that rose up to meet his booted feet now—only land, good solid land.

It was a simple and universal truth that land made a man rich, Fane conceded. A ship could sink in a few minutes, and with it a man's purse and his hopes for his future. Pay your taxes, though, and land could be yours forever. As some wag had said, "God was not making any more of it." Land made a man important, if he owned enough of it.

A man need not be clever, nor productive, nor innovative to gain the esteem of his neighbors, not if he owned a vast range of land. It was enough to own it, to be called master of it, and you would have power, deserved or otherwise. Fane knew he would be a fool to lightly dismiss the endowment, the distinction, the authority that could be his, if he were indeed his father's heir. He had thought about the possibility of inheriting while he'd sailed toward England, but that had been abstract, unreal. Standing here, now, looking at that breadth of the Galbreth domain visible even in the dim light of stars, he knew it was real enough, and could not be lightly dismissed.

The land itself was enough to seduce a man, but the title was a privilege not to be disparaged either. There were those toadeaters in America who fawned over a title as avariciously as any man, despite that nation's battle cry in the name of societal equality. It might be well and fine to talk of working for the common good, for the enlightenment of all men, but even in the midst of revolution a third of the nation had cherished the old ways, and another third had not cared which way any war might blow them, so long as they personally landed on their feet. Now, some forty years later, the Americans had just fought another war, one to protest how their one-time motherland still felt she had the right to build her navy by seizing the sons of her former colony. And even so, despite two wars, there were those ambitious parents who sent their daughters to England and the Continent, in hopes that their offspring might marry one of the titled class, might "rise above" their unaristocratic American "equals."

Yes, to become the Baron Galbreth would place Fane into a higher echelon. It would open doors that would never open to plain Mr. Westby, coffee buyer from Philadelphia. He would have cachet, money, prestige—the goals of every man were that man be honest with himself.

Fane stopped to watch the sun's first reach over the horizon, averting his direct gaze from its painfully golden touch, amazed to feel its warmth spreading despite the dawn chill, despite its great distance from the earth upon which he stood. It was a little like America in that: warming from its distance—but what fate would closer acquaintance bring? Whereas the sun would burn, Fane had begun to suspect that a return to America would chill, for what waited for him there but a grave? He had come to England, yes, to meet his father . . . but in the clarity of first light, Fane saw that, too, he had come to England to try and build himself a new life.

He laughed a little at himself. "One minute you are swearing you will return to America," he said aloud, "and the next vowing that your future is here. Which is it to be, m'boy?"

"Your father would wish you to remain, I think," came a female voice, and Fane looked up, startled, to find Miss Hampton emerging from the shadow of a nearby copse of trees. She led a horse behind her, a bulky cargo secured to its back.

"Miss Hampton," he said, thinking to remove his hat and execute a half-bow. He had heard the sound of hooves, but dismissed it as belonging to a wandering creature in some nearby pasture.

She curtsied, the movement for a moment disturbing her dark cloak, revealing a light colored gown beneath. She wore only a simple cap with one line of lace encircling her face—which was well, as he doubted he could have known her in the dim light had her features been obscured by the long brim of a poke bonnet.

"Forgive my intrusion," she said. "It was my intention to merely continue passing by, but when I heard you speak, I felt I should warn you of my presence." It was impossible to say for sure in the dawning light, but she might have blushed a little. "And it was my impudence that induced me to speak in return, to offer my opinion on what is surely a private decision."

"There was no impudence."

"Hmm. But now there shall be, for I should like to ask you a question, my lord." She spoke clearly, but in quiet tones; it would seem she did not wish her voice to carry on the early morning breezes.

"As you wish, but I am to be allowed to ask one first. How is it that you are wandering the fields at such an ungodly hour, Miss Hampton?" he asked, making his tone light.

She indicated the horse and its oil-cloth wrapped burden. "My aunt and I weave, Lord Galbreth, for the income it brings us. But everyone prefers to pretend we do not engage in such a vile thing as commerce, and so to maintain the happy illusion, I am forced to deliver my goods into the village before dawn." She spoke bluntly and looked at him square on, as if she defied him to be shocked or disillusioned at the practice.

It was the same in America. Women could engage in trade, but they earned little enough respect for doing so. It might be understood, tolerated, but it brought no sheen to a woman's standing in the community. The tea merchant's daughter might be invited to all the best parties—but not if she were seen doling out the measures from the shopfront.

"You prefer walking rather than delivering the goods in your carriage?" Fane replied instead, resettling his hat on his head. "I suppose the clatter of the wheels might disturb those who reside in the village."

Now she averted her gaze. "I have no carriage."

Fane pursed his lips, regretting the maladroit comment. "My apologies, Miss Hampton."

She shook her head, dismissing the moment. "It is my turn to ask a question, if you recall."

"Anything."

"This is not the first time I have heard you say that you are considering returning to America, that perhaps you will not accept the title your father surely left to you."

He nodded slowly.

"My question is *why?*" Her brow wrinkled. "You could accept it all, and then choose to be an absentee landlord, letting a steward manage the estate for you. The rental monies could be sent on to America, leaving you utterly free of the burdens of administrating the estate yourself, but while adding to your worth, if I may be so bold as to say. Why ever would you cast away such a boon when there is no need?"

There were a dozen answers he could give her, all of which might satisfy her curiosity. He could argue that Miss Hampton the enigma was not due any particular honesty on his part . . . except he had the uncommon feeling that in their few brief dealings Miss Hampton had never been anything but honest with him.

"Because I am a stranger here, Miss Hampton," he explained simply. At her perplexed expression, he went on. "Even if I were to take this legacy of my birth, I would still be an outsider here." He glanced to the horizon, noting the sun's slow climb upward in the sky. "So, you might ask, why not take the money and run?" He gazed back at her, seeing that her dark, almost black eyes were transformed into tiger's eye

stones by the gilding touch of the morning sun, a sight
to almost make him forget what he meant to say. "Take
the money?" he repeated. "And give my honor in exchange? I cannot live from money I've done nothing
to earn. I cannot play the part of the landed gentleman—not without seeing to the planting of that land,
to the harvesting of its crops. I cannot let others toil
in my place while I grow fat and lazy on their proceeds."

He was surprised when her mouth shaped into a
slow, dawning smile. "But no one man may plant all
the fields that belong to this estate, my lord," she
pointed out, no sting in her words.

He found himself smiling, too. "You take me too
literally."

"I know I do. I am teasing you."

It was a small, silly word, this "teasing," yet something about the warmth in her voice, the charming
curve of her mouth, the gemlike shine in her eyes,
made him aware of a sudden pronounced beating of
his heart deep beneath his greatcoat.

"It is just that I have not often had the privilege of
meeting a man who considered his honor over his
advantage," she said, and now her regard caused a
warmth to flow outward to his every limb. He suspected his face had become flushed, and was glad his
back was to the sun, that his face might be at least
partially obscured from her observation.

Her horse tossed its head, rattling its halter. Miss
Hampton absently reached to pat its neck in a soothing
gesture, but it was to Fane that she glanced. "You have
a dilemma," she said, still smiling faintly. "You will not
go if it means collecting rents you feel you have not

earned, and you will not stay because this is no home to you."

How neatly she summed it up, he thought to himself even while he nodded in accord.

"You could always choose to deny the inheritance," she told him.

"I well may."

"Do you have someone, a sweetheart, waiting for you in America?" Miss Hampton tilted her head a little to one side in inquiry.

"No." He gave a self-conscious laugh, beginning to recognize that Miss Hampton had already come to know far more about himself than he knew of her. Could it be this talent of hers, of drawing out confessions a person had not thought to make, that had somehow resulted in her banishment?

"No connections at all?"

"I have friends there, Miss Hampton, but no family. I am told I have a cousin here in England, but you must know we have never met. I will need to make inquiries to even learn his name."

"This cousin is the one in Russia," she stated. "The one who would inherit in your place." She frowned, and Fane scolded himself for being flattered at what seemed to be Miss Hampton's displeasure at the thought of the cousin inheriting.

Her horse tossed its head again, and Miss Hampton tightened her grip on the reins, sliding her hand nearer the horse's nose, the better to control the animal. "I should be going. Dawn is here already."

"Ah yes. You may be observed making your delivery," Fane cautioned, glancing at the rising sun.

Miss Hampton shrugged. " 'Tis only a polite ruse

anyway. And old news at that. I have seen for myself just now that you were not shocked to learn of my financial endeavors, and you here only two days. The villagers have long since accustomed themselves to my eccentricities."

She curtsied in preparation of leaving, but Fane put out a hand. "No, wait a moment, please. We must speak about the immediate future."

Miss Hampton slid her hands down the reins, her steady gaze dropping for once, even as the horse dropped its head to the ground to snuffle about for some greenery to eat.

"It is about the dower house," she said, and her voice was flat.

"You must realize I must ask you and your aunt to move," he said. "Your reputations—"

"Hang our reputations!" she interrupted him, and now she blushed furiously, this time with agitation. "Please, my lord, I mean no disrespect, but I must tell you that your father promised the use of the house to my aunt. I really must insist that you honor that promise."

He lifted an eyebrow at the word "insist." "You would, of course, be compensated for any moving expenses—"

"No! No, we must have the house. The dower house!"

"Why? Why not simply move to some other likely abode, Miss Hampton? You have to be aware that our proximity is a questionable matter, at best," he explained.

"We cannot move!" she cried, the sound nearly a wail.

"Why not?"

"We have no other place to which we might go."

"But surely another house might be found. No one could take it amiss if you were to require a short time to find a place—"

She would not meet his eye, turning her head to one side. Her horse took a step back, no doubt responding to the alarm in her voice, and Fane noted her hand not holding the reins was knotted into a fist at her side. It seemed unlike her to avert her gaze, and the sight of that bowed head made him step directly before her. He reached to touch one finger to her chin, and she allowed him to tilt her gaze up to meet his once more.

"Explain it to me," he said.

She sighed, a long shuddering sound full of reluctance. "It is a matter of funds, my lord," she forced herself to say, speaking even more softly than before. "Your father set no rent for us. We have lived there for free, and the very truth is that we cannot afford to pay rent elsewhere."

"Oh. I see." He thought perhaps his face had flushed as darkly as her own for effecting that confession from her. It made sense of some things, however. *We'll see that's all settled,* his father had said. Had his papa offered the ladies the dower house, as she claimed? Or had the "settlement" Father had intended been to evict the ladies? Certainly Miss Hampton, although she claimed the former, also feared the latter.

"Or rather," he said now, slowly, thinking his thoughts aloud as he dropped his touch from her chin, "I am not so sure I see. Miss Hampton, had you meant to discuss the matter of your rent with my father the day I informed you he had passed away?"

She nodded, closing her eyes for one long moment. "My lord," she said, opening her eyes again, her voice perhaps trembling just a little. "I would be entirely honest with you, if I may."

He nodded, encouraging her to go on.

"My aunt has been your father's paramour for fifteen years."

He saw the surprise register in her eyes when he nodded again.

"You knew? Oh, but of course, Bintliff would have mentioned it, I suppose," she said with a sigh. "My aunt is . . . unusual. A free spirit. She had no interest in accepting gifts. Their love was enough for her. But the rub of it all, my lord, is that your father said he meant to let her remain in the dower house all her days, but he never produced any proof that he had guaranteed that possibility," Miss Hampton said quickly, as though to get the whole story out before he could interrupt. "I meant to ask him for that proof, even though my aunt specifically said I must not."

She stopped speaking and lifted her chin. "We have not sufficient funds to rent anywhere else. We will starve or . . . or worse if we are made to move. There, you have the whole sorry truth of it all! And now I am afraid I must throw myself upon your mercy, and ask that we be allowed to continue residing there, free of rent. I vow we shall not disturb you in any way, and we shall keep the property neat and tidy, and—"

"And," now he did interrupt, "can this be the reason you said my father would wish me to remain in England? That I might agree to your request, and that you might not have to throw yourself upon the mercy of whoever should follow behind me should I surrender the inheritance?" he asked, careful to make his tone neutral rather than biting.

"No," she said, taking a step back from him. It was either the spreading light from the dawning sun or from some burning emotion within her that her eyes became lit with small dark fires of indignation, and her words were lent the ring of truth. "I said that because I think it is true. Your father spoke of you sometimes to my aunt, told her that he wished for the son he had lost, that if you lived yet he wished to be able to find you. Your father meant for this estate to be yours. Once he got your letter, his solicitors were called from London. Surely that means you were put in his will, if you were not there before in absentia. Why would your father do that if not to allow you to inherit?"

Fane waved aside the question of his possible inclusion in his father's will. "I will write to the solicitors today," he said. "We shall learn the facts soon enough. But that is not what concerns me now, Miss Hampton."

"The house," she supplied for him, her lips slimming together into a bitter line.

"The house," he agreed. He put up a hand to forestall whatever she meant to say next. "Your words have not fallen on deaf ears, Miss Hampton. After all, what do I care about that house? As far as I am concerned, you and your aunt may live on there forever if you wish."

An incredulous smile trembled around her mouth,

not quite ready to spread up into her eyes. "But?" she said.

"But how can you wish to live there, for you yourself have spoken the first of many words of condemnation sure to come your way—not to mention my own. Because we do not care for it does not mean we can will the gossip away, Miss Hampton."

Where her face had recently been flooded with color, now only two twin red ovals remained on otherwise pale cheeks as she seemingly struggled to find another actuality, and failed.

"Merciful God," she whispered, the words a prayer. Her eyes misted, but she blinked back the tears. "I cannot stay. I cannot go. What am I to do?"

He frowned, and they stared at one another, until one corner of her mouth twitched downward. She pulled up her horse's head, and half turned from Fane, seemingly a sign of resignation.

His first instinct was to assist her in some way, but his second was to recall his own uncertain state in this strange land, to say nothing of the unreliability of her claims. He should do nothing, not until the contents of the will were known—but what if that process took weeks, or months?

"Let people gossip," he growled his thoughts aloud, only to realize such gossip would little harm him, already the peculiar stranger. The people it stood to harm were Miss Hampton and her aunt.

Miss Hampton nodded in agreement, but she did not turn back to meet his gaze. It seemed that to keep a roof over her head she was willing to sacrifice the last shreds of her reputation.

If it was Miss Hampton's choice to remain, how

could Fane cast her out? After all, a poor reputation could be endured, perhaps, but to have no place to live, no home. . . . Be she a liar or a paragon, needing a home was one thing with which Fane could easily empathize.

"What if," he murmured his thought even as it formed, "Miss Hampton, what if you could do something for me?"

She appeared dubious, but perhaps there was a spark of hope in the sideward glance she sent him. "My lord?"

"What if you, and your aunt of course, were to serve as hostesses for me? I have no wife, no mother to help me, and it is clear I shall be expected to entertain to a small degree while I am here to play this part of English Baron."

"However could that make our situation seem more respectable?" she asked, but she had turned back to him, her interest caught. "Unless . . ."

"Unless?"

"Unless it was plain to everyone that I was only your employee—" She cut herself off, but Fane could see that she worked with the idea, turning it, shaping it, finding a way to make it fit her purpose.

"Tell me how, and we shall make it so," Fane said.

She gave him a look from under her lashes, as if to hide the full strength of the hope that now sparkled in her darkest brown gaze.

"There is a way. If you should make it plain that you are seeking to marry, my lord, that I am to serve only as hostess until you find a bride, then I think it could work." She quirked an eyebrow, perhaps in self-mockery. "But I cannot think you so kind as to marry simply to resolve my situation."

"A bride? Marriage?" Fane said on a frown, sure his expression must be one of alarm. "It is too early for such thoughts for me. I could not ask a woman to have me, with no idea of where my future lies. Here. Or America." He shook his head in apology. "There has to be another way."

"But if you were seen to be looking . . . and, to put no gilding on it, were seen to be indifferent to my presence. . . ." She pursed her lips, considering the possibilities.

"And, forgive me for delving into your concerns, Miss Hampton, but my valet informs me that you have a beau. If he might be persuaded to make a party with us a time or two, that it be entirely clear to one and all . . . ?" Fane suggested.

Miss Hampton blushed. "I suppose he might be persuaded . . . ?" she said, her voice rising in question.

Fane waved away her doubts. "Then it is settled. You will be my hostess, my guide to all matters English, and in exchange your aunt will have the dower house until such time as you may afford another residence."

Miss Hampton parted her lips to speak, but whatever she had meant to say, she swallowed as she nodded agreement.

"I'm afraid you must be as Caesar's wife, not only being above reproach, but *appearing* to be above reproach—a heavy burden, I should think, but one to satisfy all our needs," Fane said.

"*Your* needs, my lord? All I offer you is advice. It seems to me this is hardly a fair exchange." She was clearly perturbed.

"If I am to live here, Miss Hampton, I must be accepted. I have already rendered a dozen *faux pas*, and have understood my error in only half of those." He warmed to the words even as he thought of them. "Let us then expand your role. In addition to a hostess, I also require a tutor if I am to become what I, at least for now, claim to be—an English gentleman. I need a guide, Miss Hampton."

"You could hire a dozen instructors in the various arts," she protested.

"I do not need so much to know how to dance, as how to ask a young lady if she will dance with me! I have already learned I must not introduce myself, but what else do I not know?" He paused for a deep breath, wondering with a silent humor what he was letting himself in for. "I am not much of a believer in fate, Miss Hampton, but my homeland taught me to make the most of what comes my way. Despite the odds, we have found a way to satisfy us both. Do not turn it aside from some curious scruple. You will earn your place in the dower house, and I shall learn my way about this blighted land of yours. What say you?"

"I say you must be half-mad," she said, but she smiled as she spoke. Then she looked him straight in the eye. "My lord, I thank you."

There it was again—that curious sensation of feeling his own heart pounding.

Without waiting for a platitude of any kind from him, she turned, leading her burdened horse away, not looking back and not lowering her chin either.

He watched her go, and pondered that Miss Hampton seemed to be thoughtful and caring . . . and effective. He'd had no intention of letting her remain in the dower house. No intention of hiring a "tutor." He'd not even come to the conclusion that he would leave the legacy of Peter White behind him and start anew in this new land—and yet now Fane found himself more than half committed to that path. While Miss Hampton seemed to be all that was straightforward and honest, a part of Fane remembered that Mama had been straightforward and honest . . . and sometimes manipulative, and too often stubborn to a fault.

"What devil took hold of me?" Fane quietly asked himself, and shook his head in amusement at his own folly. He turned, the hem of his greatcoat flaring in his haste, and strode back toward the house. It seemed to him that Miss Hampton was a strong enough woman to choose manipulation, should it suit her to do so. She'd extracted a promise from him that he would be seen to court the local misses . . . but he'd be damned if he were going to choose a bride, just to suit Miss Hampton's pleasure! He had made a pledge to this stranger, this rebellious daughter, but he'd be cast into the pit before he'd allow her freedom to be bought at the cost of his own.

He ignored the thought that if a devil had indeed taken hold of him, then it could only be said that the devil came in a very engaging package.

Nine

"Why start with the tenants?" Lord Galbreth asked Marietta late the next morning. "Have I been mistaken and am now to learn that England is more likely to mix the classes than I had been raised to believe?"

Was that a curl to his lip? Marietta looked closely at Lord Galbreth's face as he handed her up into his coach, but she could not say what emotion moved him. Disdain? For her, since their odd bargain made just yesterday? For England? For the tenants he was to meet? Or could it be something to do with the way he paused and stared up at the coach driver?

She settled on the bench next to her Aunt Silvia, and Lord Galbreth entered the coach and sat across from them, a new, wide and ornate black ribbon he or his valet had tied around his hat's brim fluttering in the wake of his actions.

"Of course we must begin with the tenants, my lord," she belatedly answered his question. "Not only is it important that you learn the extent of your estate, and what it will take to manage it properly, but you must win the affections of your people."

He reached up and rapped on the coach ceiling, and leaned to the window to call out to the driver, "There we are then, Biggins! Let us be on our way, thank you." He leaned back, facing the ladies as the coach lurched forward. "My people, you say," he muttered, shaking his head. "As if I own them!"

"But America does engage in slavery, does it not?" Marietta asked, surprised by the distaste in his voice.

"Not in Philadelphia, we don't! It is America's disgrace that the institution is practiced at all. And do not give me such a wide-eyed look, for I am fully aware that England has its bondsmen, which are all but the same as slaves."

She inclined her head in a gesture that conceded the point. "I confess I thought everyone had slaves in America."

"We do not," he said indignantly.

"I see."

He turned a disgruntled gaze to the window, and something in his expression reminded her of their meeting early the previous morning. What must he think of her, not only that she would bargain her woven wares to the local merchant, but that she was so pitiable as to plead with him for a roof over her head?

She had told her aunt some of the details of yesterday's encounter, being careful to phrase the matter of Galbreth's cooperation in terms that would not offend her aunt's sensibilities as to what was fair and proper. Their housing would be in exchange for assistance rendered—a simple interchange.

"That will do very well," Aunt Silvia had said. A speculative gleam had sprung to life in her eyes. "And I believe it is just the thing for you, Marietta, to be seen more frequently out and about in Society. It has been my way to choose to be on my own and not to marry, but I do not think you are the manner of woman who wishes to end as a spinster. How can you ever find a mate if you are forever slaving away at the loom for hours on end as you do? I think this is quite the thing that we are to go out driving with Lord Galbreth."

"I . . . that is, *we* shall not be 'out driving' with Lord Galbreth. We will be riding along with him, to see to our duty as his tutor," Marietta had said firmly.

"Oh, yes, quite," had been Aunt Silvia's reply, but the speculative gleam in her eye had not faded. Ah well, let her aunt enjoy her flights of fancy about such folly as marriage for her disgraced niece—at least they chased the bereavement, however briefly, from her eyes.

Aunt Silvia certainly appeared satisfied this morning as she settled in the coach's squabs. Her pleased smile was in contrast, however, to Marietta's own emotions, which were too tangled to sort clearly in her mind. She was grateful that she need not move at once from the dower house, but also well aware that Lord Galbreth had made no long-term promise. He had sworn that Marietta's *aunt* might stay so long as the two of them met Galbreth's stipulations, but he had not included *Marietta* in that promise. She could not help but wonder if his choice of words had been deliberate. Well, it was no small thing that Aunt Silvia was guaranteed a home . . . for a while longer, at least . . . but why would Silvia not then be able to share it with Marietta . . . ?

Marietta's thoughts went around and around on the matter. Could it be that Galbreth feared that any wife he might take would object to a young woman living so close at hand? Or was it something more than that, some upper hand he meant to keep? Marietta ought to have pressed him, ought to have clarified the point—but she had known such relief at his suggested plan that his promise's lack had not struck her until hours later over supper.

And now, here was Aunt Silvia, casting smiles back and forth between Galbreth and Marietta as if she expected some wonderful affinity to spring to life before her eyes. It was only natural, Marietta supposed, that her aunt would wish to imagine hearts and roses blooming—given this man's resemblance to Silvia's own lost love—but being a natural response did not make it an agreeable one for the object of her misplaced conjectures.

It was scarcely conceivable, Marietta thought, that any respectable gentleman would look upon herself, with her straitened circumstances and ruined reputation, with such favor as to offer for her hand. There was absolutely no reason to even pretend that the handsome, unmarried, and soon-to-be well-heeled Lord Galbreth would ever care to look to the strident, penniless hoyden living practically on his doorstep for marriage, nor even for companionship. That dear Aunt Silvia could even affect such a hope, proved she was forever fashioning a happy fog in which to reside!

Her aunt's preposterous intimations could be ignored easily enough, but the fact that Marietta's knee kept bumping against that of Lord Galbreth could not. He was such a large man that although he sat up straight, there was nowhere for his knees to be but knocking against those of the ladies opposite.

Marietta found that it took a great deal of concentration to act as though she scarce noticed each small collision, and also in trying to ignore a curious tingling that spread through her each time the rocking coach caused their knees to touch. It quite made her legs prickle all the way down to her toes, the sensation not unlike the tingle that would race up her spine during a particularly moving piece of music. Marietta tried shifting her position, hoping that the change would excise the tingling sensation even if it could not keep her knee from thumping against his, only to discover the shift did not help the tingling at all.

She was so lost to schooling her features (hopefully into a mask of oblivious indifference), that it took Marietta a moment to realize Lord Galbreth had turned back to face the coach's interior. She realized she had been staring directly into his face for several very long moments, for he stared back wordlessly, but with an intensity that only served to unnerve her even further. Tingling filled her anew, this time becoming a jolt that ran right up her spine and made the tips of her ears flood with warmth.

"Er . . . there is another reason," she mumbled, shaking her head as if she could shake off her reactions. "Er, another reason why you should meet your tenants, Lord Galbreth, besides the fact they are 'your people.' "

He sighed and scowled at once, settling back in the squabs as he crossed his arms over his chest. "I cannot get used to that—the title I mean. One minute I was mere 'Mr.' from Philadelphia, and the next I had become someone whom everyone must address as 'my lord.' "

"Think of it as when you went from being 'Master

Fane' to 'Mister Westby,' " Aunt Silvia suggested, smiling encouragement at him.

Marietta raised her hand to her lips and gave a small cough to cover a smile that rose to her lips when Lord Galbreth's scowl only deepened. It seemed the trappings that came with being a member of a landed aristocracy did not sit well on Lord Galbreth's shoulders—perhaps explaining his sour mood.

"I do not even drive my own conveyance here!" he said tersely.

"Well, since it is likely going to rain, I for one am most grateful that you did not send for your phaeton just so you might finger the ribbons yourself," Aunt Silvia replied, still smiling.

"The point I was trying to make," Marietta said, interrupting whatever sharp-edged comment Lord Galbreth seemed inclined to offer her aunt, "is that if your tenants think well of you, and your farm flourishes, word will spread quickly. Society will begin to embrace you. At first only here in Kendall Town, of course—but do not underestimate the strength of local acceptance. When our little gathering of Society goes to London, they will carry word, and you will already have half the entree you require before you ever step foot in Town."

"Whoever said I wish to go to London?"

"All young unmarried men go to London." She could not help the humor that crept into her tone, for Lord Galbreth only lacked the pouting lower lip to complete the picture of the quintessential disgruntled little boy.

"Whatever for?" he demanded.

Marietta lifted a brow. "Why do young men come from the countryside into Philadelphia?"

The lessening of his scowl revealed she had made her point.

"To see the theatre, to go gaming if they have funds, and to meet other young people, I should think," she answered for him. "Just as young men with the means do here in England. Besides, you have a home in Town. You will wish to see it at some time."

"A home in London!" he shook his head, as though in disbelief of his change in status. "Presuming, of course, that I am to inherit."

"Did you write to the solicitors?"

"I did. Poole was able to give me their direction. With luck, I shall receive some manner of reply within a week."

"And have you considered hiring a new steward?"

Although he did not say aloud that her questions might be a shade too invasive of his concerns, the gaze that rested on her said it clearly enough.

"I have considered it," he answered coolly. "But since no one knows if I have any authority to do so, it behooves me to wait."

"I think not," Marietta countered at once, meeting his disapproval with a level look of her own. "Should you not inherit, then whoever does can only be grateful for anything you have put in place, so long as it profits the estate. After all, if they should not care for any action you have taken, they can undo it easily enough."

He gave a reluctant nod. "I suppose that is true enough."

"Then let us dismiss this concern over the inheritance, at least until the will should reveal a name other than your own."

He gave another nod, and then everyone's attention was drawn to the windows, for the carriage had begun to slow.

"This is where Mr. and Mrs. Burrett live. He is the head man who has been tending to your flocks since the old steward went to join his brother in an endeavor of their own undertaking," Marietta explained. Just before Lord Galbreth reached to open the door, she added, "I am afraid I must inform you that Mr. Burrett is only adequate at what he does. He means well, and the animals have not suffered—"

"But Aaron told me he had only recently realized Burrett cannot keep the books at all well," Aunt Silvia interjected. She scrunched up her face in a sign of regret. "No head for numbers, you see."

"Am I now to learn the estate is paupered because of incompetence?" Lord Galbreth asked.

"Oh, no, I should say not. But it does go to prove that you do need to find a new steward if the estate is to truly flourish," Marietta said.

Lord Galbreth's only response was to turn down one corner of his mouth in something that might be a rueful acknowledgment.

There were two dozen other introductions that followed that of Mr. and Mrs. Burrett, the tenant rounds consuming the rest of a long afternoon. But after hours of listening to his polite chatter, once back in the coach and driving homeward, Marietta had to concede to herself that Lord Galbreth had acquitted himself well. Although the tenant farmers could hardly be expected to warmly greet any newcomer, their eyes had lost a wary edge once they saw the man's physical similarity to his father and the pleasant air he put on as he greeted them. If they found his accent peculiar, they said nothing of it, and some of them even laughed at some light thing or other he said. When Lord Galbreth promised Ted Sanger that he'd have glass to replace the leather in the one window in his cottage, and the Widow Gilley that her son could come to work in his stables, Marietta saw that the tenants' words of thanks were joined by a glint of hopeful regard.

Whatever Lord Galbreth thought of the afternoon's events, he did not give voice to his impressions. He listened politely, if largely mutely, to Aunt Silvia's recitation of who lived where or owned what, as they passed each house or cottage or field, only asking specific questions now and again.

"That field, so near in to the center of the village as it is—do you call that a common? That is what we call a shared grazing area back at home," he said, indicating the broad green expanse rolling away from the road.

"Exactly so." Aunt Silvia beamed at him.

He nodded, evidently cataloguing the information, just as he appeared to have been doing all afternoon as each new thing or name was pointed out to him. All in all, this new Lord Galbreth seemed a competent fellow. Marietta would even have to say his outward show of intellect was . . . engaging. Yes, that was the word. How easy it was to think only of his recent status as foreigner, to assume the stranger must be lacking in certain graces or understanding. But there was nothing slow-witted or uncomprehending about the man, not in the way he held himself nor the attention he paid to the task at hand.

Marietta discreetly glanced at his face as he peered out the window, his profile shadowed by the angle of the late afternoon sun. His was a strong face, with less of the rounded chin and cheekbones his father had possessed, his more pronounced jaw and cheeklines perhaps being handed down from his mother. He exuded an air of confidence that contrasted markedly with the fluster he had shown her yesterday just before his father's funeral service.

As if reading her thoughts, he looked away from the window and reached into his pocket, producing the ribbon she had lent him yesterday. "Again, I thank you for this."

"You are welcome." She took it from his hand—ungloved, as she had noticed his hands often were, as it had been when he had touched his finger to her face yesterday. Had he been unable to afford gloves before now, or had he worked with his hands at tasks that made gloves unserviceable? How little she knew of him, of what his life had been until now.

He sat forward, his ungloved hands clasped. "Tell me then, Tutor Hampton, what did I do wrong today? In what way was I not the perfect English gentleman? You must spare me no blushes."

"You did very well," she said honestly. "But I did notice one thing."

"And that was?"

"You thank your servants too frequently."

He gave a short laugh. "I what?"

"You thank your servants too frequently. It is very

good of you, but the simple truth is it reveals you are unused to the presence of servants."

"Am I to pretend they are invisible?" He shook his head, one side of his mouth crooking up, as though in amazement at the thought.

"Indeed."

He gave one quick shake of the head. "Am I never to acknowledge them?"

"Well, of course you will, but not every time your coachman opens the door, nor every time you give him an instruction. You thank your servants for extra service, above and beyond their normal duties. I rather suppose it has become the custom to save one from having to say thank you all day long!"

Lord Galbreth shrugged. "I will do my best to be callously indifferent to their presence from here forward."

"Now you tease me. But you did ask my opinion."

"Am I allowed to thank *you?*"

She pursed her lips, to keep from smiling at his plaintive tone. "Of course."

"Then I thank you, and Miss Nicholson as well." He nodded to Aunt Silvia.

Silvia nodded in return. "I do hope you took no offense at our apparent disinterest in your person for most of the day, my lord," Silvia said, giving Marietta a quick but blatantly annoyed glance. Marietta began to shake her head, but Silvia charged ahead. "Marietta has told me of your bargain. I have to agree that it would scarce do should we appear too familiar in your company, of course. To a certain degree." Silvia said the words, but her expression implied she thought otherwise herself.

"Of course," he agreed, and if he found Silvia's words weighted, his expression did not show it.

The carriage began to slow, quickly coming to a halt. Galbreth reached for the door handle, but hesitated. He turned back to the ladies, and lifted his chin in a questioning gesture toward Marietta. "What follows next in our schemes to indoctrinate me as an Englishman?"

Marietta put a finger to her chin, thinking a moment. "Have you had any invitations to call upon others?"

"Some. Perhaps a half dozen of the funeral guests left their cards," he answered, and then the door was pulled open by a footman in the Galbreth livery.

"So few?" Marietta thought of the throng that had attended the funeral.

"Perhaps I am not the only one wondering if I am to inherit," Lord Galbreth stated just before he climbed down from the carriage.

Marietta waved his words away. "Well then, we will begin with those half dozen, and will make morning calls on them tomorrow. I know almost everyone in Kendall Town, but Aunt Silvia will know any others, of course." She climbed down from the carriage, her hand resting momentarily in his as he assisted her. She started to curtsy in farewell, but hesitated as she recalled one other lapse. "Have you ordered any mourning clothes yet, my lord?"

Galbreth shook his head, his black ribbon fluttering. "Although Poole said he would see to it that the local tailor calls upon me soon."

"Good. Until you have something suitable, be sure

to continue to wear your hat beribboned as you have it, my lord."

"I will."

A silence fell and went on a moment too long, but then Marietta thought to curtsy, as did Aunt Silvia. Lord Galbreth bowed in return, and as he straightened, caught up her hand again with his own. "Thank you for your assistance today," he said just before he bowed again, this time to sketch a kiss over her hand.

"Of course, my lord," Marietta said, taking back her hand as soon as it might not be constituted as rude.

"Shall I call for you at eleven tomorrow?"

"That would suit very well."

"Until then." He bowed again, and turned to climb back into the carriage. Marietta heard him rap on the roof. The carriage began to roll almost at once. Just as she meant to turn toward the house, she saw the nearest carriage window as it lowered, and then Lord Galbreth stuck his head out. "Please note I did not thank my driver!" he called with a grin.

Marietta felt an answering smile spread across her mouth, and she lifted her hand to offer him a salute. He returned it before settling within the coach once more.

"You silly girl," Aunt Silvia said, also smiling.

"Silly? Why ever do you call me silly?" Marietta turned to her aunt in surprise.

"You ought to have invited him in for tea, or at the very least you should have batted your eyelashes at him when he kissed your hand."

"I would never bat my eyelashes at a gentleman, no more than would you!" Marietta cried.

"It seems to work for other ladies. Although I con-

fess I never understood why it should," Silvia confessed.

Marietta shook her head, amused in spite of herself,
and put her arm through that of her aunt. "You and
I must have a talk, my dear," she said mock-sternly,
pulling her aunt along toward the house.

"About men?"

"About a certain man, and how I cannot, will not
set my cap at him."

"Why ever not?" Aunt Silvia asked, appearing totally undeflated by her niece's censure. "Do not attempt to tell me that you are in love with the insipid
Mr. Walker. I shan't believe it for a moment."

"I am not in love with anyone. I am in no position
to *be* in love with anyone."

"Fustian!" Silvia said with emphasis. "You are a
good girl who has had some poor luck—"

"Aunt Silvia! I very much doubt that Lord Galbreth
is about to take a serious blow to the head—and you
should know that is the only way he would consider
me as an eligible *parti*. You simply *must* desist with such
nonsensical talk."

Silvia cast up her hands as though in defeat. "Far
be it from me to tell anyone how to live their life, but
I *do* know you rather well, my dear girl, and I think
you must use to your advantage—"

"Aunt Silvia."

Silvia ceased to speak, but she added a disapproving
sniff that spoke of later arguments to come.

Marietta sighed, too wearied by the day's events to
argue for more than one night's reprieve from the
oft-discussed subject of her future prospects. The

truth was, Marietta did not have any, even if her aunt wished to pretend she did.

The same did not hold true for Lord Galbreth, should he ever truly enter into the search for a wife. But perhaps she could help him along that road, while acting as his tutor? She would look for someone pleasant, someone generous enough to think nothing of female strangers in the dower house.

Someone with either hearty knees or short legs, she added on a private smile, thinking back on her carriage ride with Lord Galbreth.

Later that evening, Fane stood with his hands on his hips as he considered the various equipages before him. He pursed his lips and shook his head.

"Walter," he said to the stable lad. "Did my father have any carriages that did *not* sport his crest?"

"Aye, m'lord. Gigs. Two of 'em," Walter replied with a nod.

"Good. Show them to me."

Walter led the way to the rear entry of the stables. The two gigs stood side by side, their shafts resting on the straw-covered floor. "There they be, m'lord."

Fane moved from one to the other, sizing up both conveyances. He pointed at the one on the right. "This one affords more room for two passengers, I think."

"Aye, it does. D'you want me to have it rigged fer you, m'lord?" Walter offered.

"No, what I want you to do is to cut a few slits in its leather seat, and then sew them back together as neatly as you may, with good strong catgut. Then I want you to splash some whitewash on it—not too much, mind you—and bring it back in for the night to dry."

Walter's jaw fell open. "M'lord?" he said in obvious disbelief. "You want me to ruin it?"

"Not at all," Fane said on a smile. "I want it to end as being presentable, but only just."

Walter gave an exaggerated shrug. "As you please, sir."

"I do please," Fane said. He grinned to himself, and turned to go back to the house, humming a light tune as he walked.

"I cannot think what to do with it," Fane said to Miss Hampton the next morning as he dismounted from his horse.

Miss Hampton glanced at the gig, then back at Fane, her head cocked a little to one side in suspicion. Her aunt stood at Miss Hampton's side, the elderly lady's hands clasped together as though in ecstatic prayer.

"I have not the room to store the gig as it ought to be stored, and yet as you can see, it is not in so poor a condition that it is ready to be consigned to the heap for extra parts," Fane explained, hoping he sounded at least vaguely authentic.

"Hmmm," said Miss Hampton. She glanced at the stableman, who was busily avoiding her gaze while he unharnessed the horse that had brought the gig along to them.

"Yes, we see your difficulty," her aunt said to Fane.

"So I was wondering if I might leave the gig here for a while, until I can decide what to do with it, or else to sell it perhaps. Of course I would expect you ladies to use it in the meanwhile, since I am asking to inconvenience you by storing the gig here."

Miss Hampton glanced at the shed that served as shelter for her horse. "The gig might fit," she conceded, "but I doubt it would escape unscathed if my gelding were ever to kick up his heels."

Fane waved away the concern. "I would not hold you responsible for any damage. So, will you be so kind . . . ?" He smiled in invitation.

"Of course we will," Miss Silvia said graciously.

Miss Hampton still looked dubious. She was no doubt wondering how it would look to the locals if she were suddenly to have a carriage at her disposal.

"It is not a gift," Fane said. Miss Hampton gazed at him, the light in her eyes confirming his suspicion. "It is a favor you are doing for me." Fane glanced at his stable lad. "Tell Miss Hampton how crowded the stable is, Walter."

Walter gripped the brim of his hat in a quick salute to the lady before his gaze slid away and he grunted a vaguely confirming noise.

"My lord—" she began.

"There! Is it all settled! I do thank you most humbly, ladies, for this service."

Fane turned without meeting Miss Hampton's steady regard, and swung himself back up into his saddle. Walter scrambled onto the back of the unsaddled horse that had drawn the gig.

Fane tipped his hat. "I shall return at eleven as I promised yesterday, and we can begin our morning calls, ladies."

"Lovely, lovely," Miss Silvia said, beaming her approval.

Miss Hampton stepped up to Fane's horse, one hand reaching to stroke its nose as she gazed up at Fane. "I only hope this 'storing' of your gig does not undo all that we work to settle," she said quietly. She flicked a glance at Walter, perhaps mindful of servants' gossip.

"I shall put about the truth of your kindness in storing it, today while we are about," Fane said.

"Hmmm," Miss Hampton said, again looking doubtful.

As he rode away, Walter following, Fane pondered that doubting look. Miss Hampton was no fool. She knew Fane had manufactured an excuse by which he could supply her and her aunt with a carriage.

She told him as much after he returned at eleven in his coach. As they stood before the dower house, waiting for Miss Silvia to exchange her wool cloak for a lighter wrap to match the fineness of the day, Miss Hampton took the opportunity to speak alone with him. "I thank you for the use of the carriage, my lord. I am sure I did not seem properly grateful before. As my aunt is going on in years, I cannot pretend I am displeased that she now may call upon her friends in comfort."

He did not belittle her words by extending the pretense that it was she who was doing the favor for him. "You are welcome, Miss Hampton."

"You are very generous, given who my aunt is . . . has been . . ."

"To my father, yes. Well, that is all water under the

bridge in the first place, and in the second, I have taken a liking to your aunt.''

Fane had not realized the truth of the words until he said them. Perhaps he had begun to like her when she had asked him to consider the recent change in his status in the light of turning from "Master Fane" into "Mister Westby." Never mind that he had never been known as "Master Fane" nor even "Mister Westby" in America—something about the woman's guilelessness had struck him. Or had it been the small laugh Miss Hampton had been forced to cover up that had charmed him? Either way, he realized he liked Miss Silvia Nicholson, whether or not she had been mistress to his father.

Now Miss Hampton smiled in response to his claim that he valued her aunt's company—and her smile was reward enough for any generosity on his part. He had noted before the particular way her smile had of transforming her interesting face into a radiant one, but the effect was no less breathtaking for all that he had witnessed it before. He was tempted to catch up her hand and kiss her fingers as he had done yesterday, but the impulse was interrupted by Miss Silvia's exit from the dower house.

Both ladies were handed up into the coach, and then Fane leaned in the door and inquired, "Who do we venture forth to call upon first?" He handed across the calling cards that had been left on his butler's salver.

Miss Hampton consulted them, and with a nod from Miss Silvia in agreement, pronounced, "Squire Mulliton and his good lady, I should think."

"Squire Mulliton," Fane told his driver, who

touched his whip to the brim of his hat in acknowledgment.

Fane climbed in the coach, and it began to roll forward. The day's unexpected warmth soon prompted him to ask if the ladies minded if the windows were opened, and as both ladies claimed it would be lovely, he proceeded to open the windows. He settled back against the squabs, the fresh air fluttering the black ribbon that remained on his hat. "Is it far to Mulliton's?" he asked.

"A bit," Miss Hampton answered. "Which gives me time to tell you that favorable rumors are already circulating concerning yesterday's calls you made on your tenants."

"Already? How came you by this news so soon?" he asked. He resettled on the seat, angling his legs just so that his knees came into frequent contact with those of Miss Hampton as the coach bumped along. He had noted her subtle attempts to avoid his touch, and her careful but false indifference to the contact yesterday, and some devil in him urged him to repeat the unspoken dance today.

"Mrs. Bierce came to call early this morning," Miss Hampton said, shifting her legs away from his.

"She had it from Mrs. Ulridge that Ted Sanger is that pleased with your offer to put glass in his window to help keep out the winter cold when it comes, and she knows for a fact that the Widow Gilley's singing your praises for having employed her boy," Miss Silvia supplied.

Fane nodded. "He came to the stables this morning, I understand. Walter thinks he can make something of the lad."

"And even Mr. Burrett is not overset, because of your promise to keep him on as your animal master under whoever becomes your steward, of course," Miss Silvia went on.

She leaned forward, putting her hand over Fane's. "You remind me, dear boy, of your father when he was younger. He had a way about him, too, of bringing out the best in his workers, even though some called him gruff." Her features crumpled and her eyes filled with tears. "Gruff enough to think he could spare me some of the pain of his passing by keeping me away in his final days, the silly old fool!" she said, her voice thickening with unshed tears.

Fane met Miss Hampton's gaze over her aunt's head. She appeared concerned—perhaps that her aunt's tears would seem inappropriate to him. He shook his head once, denying whatever care worried her.

He put his hand over Miss Silvia's. "It might comfort you to know that he spoke of you that last night."

"He did?" Miss Silvia wiped at her eyes with her gloved hand.

"I did not realize who 'Silvia' was, of course, but I recall that he said he feared he was dying, and he re-gretted sending 'Silvia' away. I thought he spoke of the maid or housekeeper, at the time."

Miss Silvia began to weep, silently, her hands cover-ing her face, but after a minute she sniffed shakily, wiped at her face, and recovered her poise. "Whatever will the squire think of me, all puffy and red about the eyes?" she said on a brave little half-laugh, and Fane realized anew that he truly had come to value the lady's company. Whereas aunt and niece were both plain-speaking and straightforward in their approach to life, the aunt was refreshingly clear and void of pretense. Miss Hampton, for all that she looked one directly in the eye, hid her thoughts; it was no easy thing to guess at what lay behind that steady, deflecting gaze of hers.

To change the subject, Fane suggested gently, "Tell me about this weaving you do, Miss Silvia."

"That's right. You know our little secret," Miss Silvia said. She wiped at her eyes one last time, and proceeded to describe how her niece taught her about dyes and how to set them in the wool, about how to card and spin, and how the ladies were planning to expand their endeavors to encompass designs for pretty little woolen reticules. "Marietta does the cutting and sewing, and the fixing on of buttons. I am afraid my needlework is not half so clever or neat as hers."

Miss Hampton looked out the window, but Fane was fairly certain she listened to the conversation. It could not be an easy thing for her, to have come down in life as she surely had, to go from the daughter who would marry and command her own servants, to practically being a servant herself.

He shifted his seat again, this time taking care to avoid her knees, for it suddenly seemed unkind to tease her, however silently.

"We are teaching Hetty Dewlap—you met Mr. Dewlap yesterday, the brick layer?—how to spin and weave. We cannot afford to pay her, I fear, but she is learning the craft. Her mama passed away several years ago, so she has no one to teach her, even though she has a spinning jenny at home. We let her take some of the wool and use it for her papa and her, of course, dear girl. She has a twisted foot, always had it, so I fear she will not marry. A countryman requires a strong wife, after all. But she is happy to be providing what she can for her papa, and if the demand for our shawls and reticules should happen to increase, it is our dearest wish to then pay Hetty for her services," Miss Silvia said.

Now it was Fane's turn to look out the window, for he could find no words for a reply. Here were two women, by all evidence struggling to survive themselves, offering what little extra they had to the local charity case? He could only believe Miss Silvia's words, for he had already decided she was a guileless creature, but was her niece of the same stamp? Or was Miss Hampton's gaze deliberately fathomless, that others might not know what dark secrets she hid here in Kendall Town? She loved her aunt—that much she could not hide—and feared what would become of Miss Silvia should they suddenly find themselves cast from their present home. There was strength in Miss Hampton, but strength in a woman was not always a pretty, polite thing. Fane's mama was proof enough of that.

Was he a fool to allow himself to feel admiration for these ladies . . . for Miss Hampton?

"Ho!" came the driver's call, at which the carriage slowed.

"Squire Mulliton's, I presume?" Fane said, using the words as a way to shift from his uncomfortable thoughts.

"It is indeed," Miss Silvia confirmed.

"Any last words of advice?" Fane asked Miss Hampton as he climbed out of the coach.

She gave him her hand. "If you eat anything, do not commence to pick your teeth with your knife," she suggested, and only then did she grin to show it was meant as a jest. "I hear that is the practice in America."

"It is not. They pick their teeth with animal bones," Fane said archly as he assisted her down from the carriage.

His reward was to hear Miss Hampton giggle—a sound every bit as delightful as her smile.

He was slow to let go of her hand, and even slower to follow her in through the door Squire Mulliton's butler had pulled open upon their arrival. What was he to make of the reluctance that came over him at the idea of surrendering the whole of Miss Hampton's attention?

Ten

The morning calls had gone well, Fane decided as he saddled his horse two days later. He had been cordially, if not warmly, invited to take a cup of tea at each house where they stopped, and at the end had been invited back in the future. He had let it be known his own days for receiving callers would be Tuesdays and Thursdays, and when he apologized for having no card to give her, Squire Mulliton's wife had given him the name and direction of her own preferred cardmaker. It seemed that perhaps the rituals of the drawingroom in England were not so different after all than those in a drawingroom in Philadelphia, Fane concluded.

Walter waited patiently nearby, already accustomed to his new master's singular habit of saddling his own horse, and Charlie Gilley held his horse's head for Fane while he mounted.

"Past the dower house and through the copse?" Fane asked Walter now.

The stableman nodded. "And then a mile on, m'lord. That's where you'll find the sheering house, sure enow."

He started to verbally thank the man, then remembered Miss Hampton's counsel. Instead he nodded a thanks, even as he gave young Charlie an encouraging smile as the boy handed up the reins.

By human measure, it was a five minute walk to the dower house from the estate house, but the horse beneath Fane was in no mood for even so slow a pace as an equine walk, and so Fane let her break into a trot. In under two minutes they had the dower house in sight. Fane noted a lack of smoke coming from the chimney, and felt an unexpected sense of disappointment to think the ladies might not be at home.

He wished to continue his evaluation of Miss Hampton, of course, that was why he felt such disappointment. He would solve the enigma, if it was the last thing he did in England. It seemed to him Miss Hampton was the key to several puzzles: who and what she was; whether Fane would elect to stay or to go; how the estate might be best handled for all concerned.

Curious, that. Fane grinned to himself as he rode on, for he had realized the enigma was also a part of the solution.

He was still thinking of her when he reined his horse to a stop before the only building in the farmost corner of his estate. There was a gig and its single horse there before him already. Fane recognized it at once.

Anything Miss Hampton might choose to do ought not surprise him anymore, Fane thought as he dismounted and entered the estate's sheep-sheering house, but surprise him again she had, for she stood within the humble building. Surely this was no place for a lady.

"My lord!" she cried upon his entrance, and it would seem she was equally surprised to find him in this place.

"Miss Hampton," he said, doffing his hat in a quick salute before replacing it on his head. Fane noted her gloves were off, tucked under one arm, and she stood before a table piled high with sheered wool. Under her rose-hued shawl, her pink round gown was better suited to a stroll in the park than a visit to a sheering shed. It occurred to him that she had surely brought the gowns she had once worn for a London Season with her here into banishment, where the fine fabrics and delicate construction no doubt proved woefully inadequate for the countrified life she now led.

"What are you doing here?" she asked, as if she were the property owner and not the other way around.

"I could ask the same of you," he said, striding forward as he pulled off his own riding gloves.

She blushed. He had seen her blush before, but the edge of embarrassment that made her gaze slide away from his made him regret his question, so he chose to answer hers. "I have been evaluating the property, in addition to the rounds I made with you and Miss Silvia. This was the last bit I had yet to see."

"Oh, of course," Miss Hampton said, raising her eyes to meet his once more. Up went her chin, her inevitable gesture when she thought she might be censured. "I came here to buy more wool, for my weaving."

Fane glanced about, seeing across a straw-covered courtyard that a man approached an opposite double doorway, his arms piled high with more fleece. "I should think you would buy it farther from home," he said to Miss Hampton in a low voice.

Miss Hampton glanced toward where the man approached. "But I only recently obtained a carriage, my lord," she said, glancing back at Fane with a slight smile, her embarrassment giving way to a self-deprecating humor. "To travel farther afield would have been a difficult day's travel on my poor aging steed. Especially since your man here, Davey, offers me a fair price." Davey entered the building as she finished speaking, and smiled at her before he tossed the trailing armload of fleece on the top of the pile already on the table. "Besides, Davey's only trade with gossips is to ask how much they will pay for his wool. Your wool actually, my lord."

"Fane," he said. "As you are now my tutor, you must feel at ease to call me Fane."

Miss Hampton blushed anew. "Oh, I—! I do not think that would suit, sir."

"Then I am stuck with 'Galbreth'? And such a melodious name it is, too." Fane made a face. "But I suppose I must become accustomed to it. At least when we are not in public you must drop the 'Lord' part—agreed? And does this mean I may now call you just 'Hampton'?"

"Your colonial manners are showing again," she said, her lips twisting to something just short of a grin.

"I will allow you to believe that if you wish, Miss Hampton."

"I vow I am disappointed to have the 'miss' restored."

Davey looked from one to the other, his expression mildly amused and largely perplexed. Fane forced himself to turn from his light banter with Miss Hampton, and sought an introduction to the man he quickly learned was master of the sheering house.

"It's that glad I am to meet the old master's son," Davey declared with a tip of his soft woolen cap. He sized up Fane, no doubt wondering what changes the new master brought with him.

Davey's introduction led to a bargaining session over the fleece, during which Fane learned that Miss Hampton preferred the whiter, softer variety over the darker, coarser fleece also available.

"Aunt Silvia and I can achieve more colors dyeing the whiter wool," she explained to Fane. "Although I do like the coarser wool for some of the winter shawls we have fashioned."

He nodded, watching how her fingers combed through the curly fleece, examining with silent intensity the quality and texture. She pulled a tuft of the fur apart, making the hairs separate into strands which she then rolled between her fingers, wordlessly contemplating the wool's attributes. The embarrassment she had shown at first, at being caught out in the midst of once again engaging in trade, either evaporated or was pushed aside, as she went on to declare which portions she would take and what she would pay for them.

Davey looked to Fane. "Here now, m'lord, will you be taking my word 'tis a fair price Miss Hampton be proposing?"

"Since the estate has obviously yet to be beggared, I have to assume you know whereof you speak," Fane answered lightly.

He glanced at Miss Hampton, and felt a striking satisfaction when he saw she spared no more blushes on the matter. She'd had business she'd needed to conduct, and he could well imagine her thinking that the devil could take him if he thought any the less of her for it. Would she laugh if she knew he thought just the opposite?

Miss Hampton paid the fee, and Fane ignored the impulse to pay in her stead. That made no sense to pay himself—and Miss Hampton would not thank him for it anyway, not to judge by the prideful set of her shoulders as she counted out the coins.

"I'll have the lot bagged into a woolsack and brought 'round to the dower house, shall I, same as usual?" Davey offered.

"Yes, please, but—" Miss Hampton began.

"But you'll be wanting a small parcel to take with you now," Davey finished for her with a grin.

She smiled in return, and Fane saw its charm work on Davey just as it did on Fane himself, for the man cleared his throat, and nodded his head, and backed away as though to move out of the radiantly powerful circle an angel might cast. That smile was, make no mistake, the reason the villagers turned a blind eye to Miss Hampton's dealings in commerce, for to reject her was to reject any chance to bask in the glow of her smile.

"I will carry that out," Fane offered when Davey returned with a paper-wrapped bundle of fleece, about the size of a small valise, from the backroom. His offer surprised a look from both Miss Hampton and Davey. "I have helped to load many a ship. I think I can handle one bundle of sheep's wool, no matter how aristocratic my blood has suddenly become."

He was glad he'd left his riding gloves in his pocket, however, for once he'd placed the bundle in the foot-well of the gig, he felt the greasy residue that had seeped even through the paper, marks left by the un-washed wool. Bintliff would no doubt cluck in aggra-vation when he saw the marks on the shoulder of Fane's coat where he'd hoisted the bundle.

"Oh dear." Miss Hampton noted the marks. "But this should wash out," she added as she reached to brush the shoulder of his coat. She had yet to don her gloves, and Fane stiffened for a moment at the feeling of her touch. He did not want to move, for he knew she would withdraw her hand, and he was not ready to let go of the strange sensation that washed through him.

"Yes?" Miss Hampton inquired, pulling back her hand.

"Yes?" he echoed rather stupidly.

"Your expression . . . I thought you meant to say something."

"I did," Fane answered at once, casting about in his mind for some inane thing to say. "I have had word of the solicitors. Not from them, but of them."

"Oh?"

"Yes. I have had a man in this morning, a detective. He is looking for my cousin, whose name I discovered is Malcolm Westby." Fane blinked, taking a step back, as if the motion would help to clear his thoughts. "He, er, this Malcolm fellow is my father's brother's only surviving son. It seems I've just the one cousin, at least in the line to inherit. There are some remote females in Cornwall, if I read my DeBrett's correctly."

He shook his head, sure he was boring Miss Hamp-ton, although he could not know it by her attentive expression.

"No matter. This detective informs me that he's

pleased enough to investigate anywhere but in London, for it seems the influenza is rampant there just now. This fellow has a connection with Brown, Harding and Hopkins—my father's solicitors, you see. He says the two elder partners are abed, quite ill, and more than half the office staff ill as well. He tells me it may be weeks before a representative can see to forwarding the will, let alone having anyone call upon me here."

"Then I suppose you must wait," Miss Hampton said reasonably.

"I could go to London myself. 'Tis not even a two hour drive from here."

"You mustn't!" Miss Hampton said, and Fane was gratified by the alarm in her voice. "What is a few weeks' wait compared to the loss of your health?"

"Perhaps you are right," he conceded.

"Besides, there is sufficient business at hand to occupy you until word may come, I should think," Miss Hampton said, glancing about at the recently shorn sheep that grazed in the fields all around them.

"Indeed," Fane answered, but he did not think of sheep, nor of crops. He thought of a mysterious young woman who lived in his dower house, and bought his fleece, and made him grow still of a sudden by the simple touch of her hand.

The conversation over, he ought to step back and out of the way of her carriage. Instead he remained still, within arm's reach of her, as she sat back to pull on her gloves. Only then did he move, to hand her the reins, which she arranged in her hands as he moved to take her horse's bridle and lead the animal in an arc, so that now the gig was positioned to return Miss Hampton home.

"Thank you," she called with a nod of her head. Then she flicked the reins, and the gig pulled away.

"You are most welcome," he responded, but he doubted she heard him over the rattle of the gig's harness.

Fane turned to his horse, but before he mounted he rotated his shoulder, the one she had touched, as though to chase out a crick. There was no pain, just a peculiar twinge that did not go away at once.

For a moment he considered catching up to her, but then he recalled they had agreed to attend Squire Mulliton's card party tomorrow night. No need to impose his constant company upon her . . . no need at all.

Instead he followed well behind her trail, although he frequently spotted the gig when it rose out of some gully or other in the landscaping. She was not a timid driver, seeming quite comfortable with managing the carriage and the animal that pulled it—another sign that she had once led a privileged life.

"Perhaps I should have that detective discover exactly what brought you out of London, Miss Hampton," Fane spoke aloud to the back of the distant lady's bonnet. He frowned, and shook his head, not caring for the idea. "Perhaps I should just ask you directly," he added, and liked the idea as soon as it occurred to him. She would be direct in her response—even if her response was to tell him to take his questions to perdition, he thought on a grin.

In the distance, Miss Hampton pulled the gig to a stop. Fane reined in his own horse abruptly, momen-

tarily alarmed that something was wrong. Had she broken a wheel? He was just about to put his heels to his
horse once more, to urge it into a gallop, when he
spied another rider approaching Miss Hampton.
There, on the other side of the gig. Fane narrowed
his eyes, but all he could discern was the rider was a
man. That would have been even more alarming but
for an errant breeze that carried the sound of Miss
Hampton's laugh to Fane's ears.

So Miss Hampton knew the man, or at least certainly
felt no alarm in his presence, to judge by her laughter.
But only look, now she proceeded on, and the man
turned his horse around to return the way he had just
come, accompanying her as she drove. It appeared
that the two of them chatted back and forth, yet another indication of familiarity. If the man had spotted
the bundled wool sitting beside Miss Hampton's feet,
he did not affront the lady by commenting on it—
either that or Miss Hampton, as usual, refused to be
cowed by anyone else's opinion of her affairs, for her
laughter carried again on the breeze. The two proceeded on with apparent goodwill.

So then, was this man Miss Hampton's beau, the
one Bintliff had mentioned? The fact the man had
turned from whatever errand he was about in order
to accompany Miss Hampton seemed a strong indica-
tor of partiality. That was all to the good, surely, especially if the man should marry Miss Hampton. Once
wed, the lady need not be concerned as to how she
would keep a roof over her head, and surely her aunt
would be welcome to join the new household.

"That would solve everyone's problems," Fane said
to himself. He'd only have to secure whatever infor-

mation the detective garnered on this Cousin Malcolm, determine if the man were to be trusted with the care of a large estate, and presuming Malcolm was of the proper ilk then Fane would be free to sail where he would.

His horse sidled under him, protesting having stood too long. Fane dropped his hands and heeled the animal's sides, letting the horse stretch its legs in a canter. Yes, Fane thought as he rode, Miss Hampton's marriage would be a solution to many a problem.

It would be a shame, though, if an individual such as Miss Hampton found herself espoused to some country bumpkin incapable of recognizing or appreciating her obvious keen mind, her verve, her innate dignity. Fane felt a deep scowl forming on his face, and he did not try to erase it. Instead he decided, on the moment, that since he must remain in England at least long enough to investigate this cousin of his, he would make sure his time was also otherwise well spent. He would see for himself what manner of man this beau of Miss Hampton's was. Miss Hampton had already promised to do what she could to persuade the fellow to join them on some of the social rounds.

If the man was found to be inferior, however, Fane would do his best to utilize this supposed rank of his to see that the fellow was sent packing.

Eleven

"Ah, welcome! Welcome, Lord Galbreth," Mrs. Mulliton trilled as she approached Fane, who had just been announced by the butler. "Do come join our merry gathering."

She led him across her large drawingroom to where a dozen other guests were already gathered around tables arranged near a large stonework fireplace. Fane was fairly certain he had met everyone in the room before, at his father's funeral, but hoped he would not be put to the test when it came to recalling all their names. He would have to keep his ears open for clues as the guests addressed one another, he thought as he exchanged murmurs of greeting and nods of heads, for in addition to these people's faces having all blended together the day of the funeral, Fane understood only some facets of the title system of England, the particulars often escaping him. His mother had tried once or twice to instruct him in the finer points, but the subject had never held his interest.

"Titles are of the old ways, Mama," he had told her. "Have you not heard? The Frenchman and the American are done with the trappings of an aristocracy. Here a man is important because he has made himself so, not because he was born into favor."

Mama had merely sniffed at Fane's opinions, and later tried again to teach him "the old ways," for she believed such things were the way of the world, "other than a few self-indulgent Colonials and some pretentious French rabble."

Fortunately, Fane thought as he studied the vaguely familiar faces around him, the sobriquets of "ma'am" and "sir" were never inappropriate. And Miss Hampton could help guide him from going too far afield . . . but he saw in a glance that Miss Hampton was not among their number.

As if his thoughts had conjured her, the butler then announced Miss Hampton, along with her aunt. Fane could not quite stop the sigh of relief that relaxed his shoulders upon the appearance of his tutor, even as Miss Hampton had promised. She looked very fetching in a creamy-white day gown overlaid by a rose-colored pelisse, and he would wager the matching reticule of woven rose threads she carried was of her own manufacturing. The rosy pattern incorporated the occasional pearl-like bead, and the overall match between gown, pelisse, and reticule had a finished, polished look. Miss Hampton was either bold as brass to show off her new line of wares in this company, or else clever as a fox to let others see them to advantage. Fane would wager on the latter, and that Mr. Hissop the shopkeeper would soon be taking requests for his "secret" manufacturer to fulfill.

"Lord Galbreth," said a matron sitting near where Fane stood.

He turned to her—what was her name? Mrs. Ghattle? Gheddly? "Ma'am?" he inquired.

She leaned toward him, her face friendly. "May I extend my condolences on your father's passing once again?"

Fane nodded in acknowledgement. "Thank you. May I ask you something, ma'am? Can you tell me if I might be offending anyone by the fact that I am not practicing deep mourning." He had wondered if he ought to accept tonight's invitation for cardplay, but the truth was he did not have the time to spare for six months of declining all but a select few invitations.

"Oh, no, I am sure we all understand," the woman replied with seeming sincerity. She did not point out that Fane had scarcely known his father, but the fact did make it easier to excuse his behavior, Fane knew.

"My lord, I understand your mother has also passed away." At Fane's nod, she went on. "I wanted you to know I was a compatriot of Margaret's. We attended Miss Heathfax's School for Young Ladies for the same two years. I quite remember her as the most lovely and delightful girl."

The woman had succeeded in capturing Fane's regard. "Indeed?" he said, hearing the bright tone in his own voice. It was an unexpected pleasure to meet someone who remembered his mama. It was somewhat difficult to imagine Margaret White Westby as a "delightful girl," but not so difficult to allow that once upon a time she would have been a more carefree and less wounded creature. While it was true that the vagaries of life had never completely extinguished Mama's laughter, they had certainly left shadows to linger in her eyes. "I fear I do not recall if my mama ever mentioned you or not. But perhaps she would have known you better by your maiden name?"

"Oh my yes, I suppose she would have, for I married a year after dear Margaret. She might not have recalled that I married Mr. Gatheby. Did she ever mention Eugenia Oglethorp?"

Now he had her name. "I seem to recall a tale or two of a school miss named Eugenia, yes," Fane said, even though he would have been hard pressed to recite those tales now.

"Do you know, you sat upon my lap as an infant," the woman went on with a smile.

Fane felt a tinge of blood rise into his cheeks, and he cast about for a response, but decided that questioning if he had been responsible for staining a gown or two some twenty-four years ago would scarce serve. Instead he looked to where Miss Hampton stood speaking with Squire Mulliton, and wished she would come and smooth the conversation as was her forte.

Mrs. Gatheby followed his gaze. "Ah, our other new neighbor, Miss Hampton," she noted. "Poor dear."

"Why do you say that?" Fane asked at once, too eager for the answer to regret encouraging the woman to gossip.

"Well," Mrs. Gatheby dropped her voice to near a whisper, "she had an incident in her past, you see. I understand she was scarce to blame, but the family was not at all lenient. She is rusticating here among us, you see. Three months now."

"Blame?" Fane glanced at Miss Hampton, who was happily engaged in conversation and unaware she was the object of gossip. "What do you mean?" he responded in an equally low voice.

"I do not know the nature of the difficulty that sent her out of London, but she seems all that one could wish in a young woman, and her aunt absolutely dotes on her." Mrs. Gatheby's voice dropped even lower. "It must have been something to do with a broken heart, either hers or his, do you not suppose?"

"His?"

"Oh, there's never been a name linked to hers, but one has an instinct for these things, does one not?" Mrs. Gatheby clicked her tongue. "Such a handsome girl, if one likes strong features, and her dark eyes are very lovely. It seems a shame she must hide her light under a bushel here in Kendall Town."

Mrs. Gatheby prattled on, moving from the subject of Miss Hampton to a variety of other personages about the room. Before too long, Fane made his excuses and slipped away, far less interested in the general talk of babies born, cattle bought, daughters debuting, and all the other kind of newsmongering to be found in any other village in the world.

He moved through the room, choosing to avoid Miss Hampton even though she cast him several inquiring glances. His interest had been piqued, and he decided he would make some discreet inquiries regarding the lady, so he could hardly have her at his side.

Probe as he might, however, he was gratified to discover that nary a whisper stirred on the matter of Miss Hampton's source of income. It seemed a combination of a blind eye and a certain discretion on Miss Hampton's part had kept the secret largely intact. Perhaps because the matter was as harmless as it was necessary for the ladies, it had never resulted in the ostracism that surely would have occurred in London or Philadelphia, or any other larger city for that matter. Although, Fane modified the thought with an interior smile, this was hardly the cream of Society in which he found himself, not if the heir apparent to the local barony—himself—was the measure.

But that was not entirely kind of him. The truth was that these people had surprised him, had been more forgiving and welcoming than he ever would have expected. The British were tolerated in America (after all, many a man or his parents were British-born), but underneath the toleration bubbled a resentment that could not be denied. Perhaps not so much resentment, really, but a fierce, young pride, a determination to hold onto the nation they had spent forty years and more forging out of a colonial wilderness. Fane had grown to manhood in the midst of rebellion and change, had learned to scowl upon the bright red army and dark blue navy coats that frequently filled his city's streets, had called himself an American and had adopted their flatter accents, even though his mother had never let him forget he was British-born.

Even in his journeys as a coffee-buyer, Fane had seen the effects of English rule, of British imperialism and how its harsh intrusions could work to ruin native ways, native lives. Little in his experience had given Fane a reason to love the Englishman, but had instead prompted him to suspect those whose loyalties were still tied to a king's commands.

He admitted to himself now, however, that his expectations of finding in England an exaggeration of all of man's foibles and prejudices had been misplaced. He could see for himself that these English, these people of his blood, were as capable of kindheartedness as were any people anywhere. They might make allowances for him, a man who presumably stood to inherit land and money and the influence to go with them—but they had no such compulsion to be tolerant of the hapless Miss Hampton or her eccentric aunt. That they accepted both women said much for them. Although, Fane grinned to himself, "hapless" was hardly the word for Miss Hampton. It was entirely possible that no one was immune to the unnerving sway of her steady regard coupled with her devastatingly charming smile. But fair was fair, so he had to acknowledge to himself that cruelty and kindness knew no borders, and Fane felt abashed that he had allowed himself to harbor such ignorant thoughts about this isle, this England.

"You have done an admirable job of avoiding me, Galbreth," came a voice at his elbow.

Fane turned at once, already recognizing the speaker as Miss Hampton even before he could meet her near-black eyes. He mentally shook his head, hoping he wiped any vestiges of his chagrined revelations from his expression.

"I fear, however," Miss Hampton went on, "that the tattlemongers will begin to think you are *too* heedless of my presence. They will start to think the very opposite of what we wish," she reprimanded gently.

"You will have corrected that perception by approaching me as you have, I should think," he answered, deliberately making his tone light. "You are correct, though, and so must now take my arm so we may circle the room, that we might be seen together in casual but indifferent conversation. I see the players grow restless, ready to have at their cards. Come, tutor, and whisper all the various names I ought to know. We have very little time left before the play begins."

"That is hardly my fault," Miss Hampton pointed out.

"You smile very sweetly, my dear Miss Hampton, but I can hear your words are edged with sarcasm."

"Sarcasm is, in my experience, usually earned by its target."

"Do stop pricking my conscience, cruel muse, and tell me the name of that barrel-chested fellow standing by the pianoforte."

Fane caught the sound of a giggle that had started before Miss Hampton could quite gain mastery over the impulse. It was another part of her appeal, of course, that such a deep and serious creature could produce such a lighthearted sound.

"That is Mr. Harper," she answered his question. "His wife has not accompanied him tonight. They are expecting their third child, in the next month, I believe."

"Ah yes, I recall him now. Harper. Wife in the family way. I have the details in mind now. And the youth with the exceedingly high collar points? There, warming his hands before the fire?"

"That is Tobias Shreever. He is on holiday from Oxford at present."

" 'On holiday' in the middle of a school session, for I assume the sessions are much as they are in America? I think not. I think you are too kind as to say the lad was sent down for bad behavior."

"Not sent down, no. He will be allowed to return . . . but not for six more weeks, I am afraid."

Fane paused in his strolling long enough to give Miss Hampton a quick smile.

She appeared faintly puzzled by the salute as they resumed their stroll, but then she had no way of knowing that Fane was gratified by her rejection of a chance to gossip. She had been a victim of gossip herself, and now she did not mete it out. Most people would, whether they'd felt its sting or not—and some would lash out as viciously as they themselves had been struck.

Could he really have wondered, not more than a couple of days ago, if Miss Hampton was purposefully manipulative, Fane asked himself. She was clever enough to be devious, if she wished, but he was coming to believe she did not deploy any such cruel leverage over her associates. Then . . . what did she want? A roof, a bed, a full larder, of course. But there was more to Miss Hampton than mere subsistence, he was convinced of that. What dream shone out through those dark eyes of hers? What could make a hothouse flower, an entity nearly as alien here as was Fane himself, thrive in the open of the backwater that was Kendall Town?

"Miss Hampton—" Fane began to speak, even though he had no notion of what he would say, how he would solicit . . . what? Dialogue? Explanations? Friendship?

"Mr. Walker," intoned the butler, announcing a late arrival.

Fane spun at the name, his ears ringing with the title "Mister" rather than "Captain." The title made no difference, however, for the man now being greeted by Mrs. Mulliton was unmistakable in his appearance, even though he wore civilian clothes rather than a naval uniform. His hair was still cut full and brushed back into lavish waves, his posture still militarily straight, his face the same as the one that too often haunted Fane's dreams.

"Walker!" Fane said in a choked voice.

He looked down at Miss Hampton, who had grown two pinkish streaks along her cheekbones, for someone near them had whispered too loudly, " 'Tis Miss Hampton's beau."

Beau? Walker! Miss Hampton's beau? The words flashed through Fane's mind with the dizzying effect of a rifle ball grazing his temple. He did not believe the words, could not believe them . . . until he looked again at the twin spots on Miss Hampton's face, and knew the awful words were true.

Fane looked back to where Walker stood greeting his host and hostess, and with his blood thundering against his eardrums, remembered every nuance of the secret the two men shared.

He'd first seen Walker when the man had come from his captain's quarters aboard the man-of-war, *HMS Valiton,* to survey the line up of prisoners in which Fane stood tied. That had been over a year ago—back when Fane still told the greater world his name was Peter White, back when he'd yet harbored the "nickname" of Fane as a private familiarity between mother and son.

A rope had been looped around Fane's neck, not too tight—that is, not dangerously tight unless he were to lower his lashed wrists, bound by the same rope, from where they were caught together just below his chin. It would tighten, too, if the man to his right, equally bound by a segment of the same rope, were to try and move away from Fane's side. Should the line of thirty men be so foolhardy as to move as one to jump over the ship's rail, most would be strangled by the rope's pull as they fought to swim, and the rest would drown, pulled down by the tangle of rope and the terrible weight of those among them who did not know how to stay afloat.

No one was so foolhardy. Neither had they been reckless of their lives when their captors, British naval swords and pistol aimed, had forced them into long-boats to make the brief crossing over to the *Valiton.*

"Gentlemen!" Walker had said in ringing tones, that all might hear. He took a stand before Captain Powell, whose merchantman ship had been captured not thirty minutes past. "In case you have not the wit to realize it, I now inform you that you have been pressed into service in His Majesty King George the Third's Navy."

One man dared to groan a protest, and received a hard cuff to the ear for his troubles.

"His Majesty sees fit to issue his impressed men pay packets, so you will have incomes to send home to whatever harlot and brats you call your family. So, you see you have little enough cause to grumble at your fate," Walker went on.

" 'Course we can grumble," Captain Powell spat out. " 'Tis against your own laws to capture a ship or to impress men who are not British in origin." Powell flicked his eyes over the line of men secured on either side of him. "These men were all born on American soil."

Walker gave a slow, cold smile. "You try to disguise your accent, Captain, but I find I cannot believe that you never began your days on English soil."

Captain Powell flushed a dark red, in stark contrast to the bloodless hands tied together at his throat. "Nor did I say I had! So press me if you will, but these other men are exempt."

"Dear me," Walker said, beginning to sound bored. "The problem is that so many have tried to disguise their origins, I find I cannot trust any system for weeding out the liars from the more honest men. Besides," he smiled coolly again, "our countries are at war. Having yourself been a captain, you must surely realize that all rules are meant to be broken during times of war." He paused as if a thought had just struck him. "You see, I very much doubt the Admiralty, let alone His Majesty, would mind that I err on the side of providing thirty-odd more sailors for our war efforts."

Fane very much doubted that the words or the wrongful impressment of men were anything new to Walker.

"I protest—!" Captain Powell began, but he got no further before Walker struck him hard across the face, causing a trickle of blood to well from Powell's lip.

"Does anyone else care to protest? No? Then listen well! What's done is done, gentlemen. You have no choice. You are now sailors in the Royal Navy. It can be a good life, and I can be a fair man, but only if you understand you are now under my command!" He pointed to Powell, and said over his shoulder, "Ames! Cast this man overboard."

Powell struggled and kicked as he was cut from the looping rope, and some of his men cried out in dismay or tried to kick back the half dozen sailors who man-handled Powell into submission, only to receive blows and curses or to choke as the loops around their necks were pulled tight by their own efforts or the hard yank of a growling sailor.

"Wait!" Fane cried out, but he was not heard over Powell's howling protest. "Wait!" he said again, his voice a scream.

Walker turned his head at the sound, and held up one hand to halt the sailor's progress toward the rail, their struggling prisoner now held suspended helpless between them. Without looking at the two men who made choking noises where their nooses had tight-ened, Walker strolled to stand before Fane, casually ordering as if to the air, "See that those men do not choke themselves. Not quite yet anyway."

Two of his sailors sprang to carry out his order, and the two men were soon able to cough and wheeze, now able to draw in some much needed air.

"Wait for what?" Walker said as he stood before Fane and crossed his hands behind his back in a casual pose.

"There's no need to kill Captain Powell," Fane said, struggling to control the white-hot fury burning in him. "And it's no way to win our loyalty."

"Loyalty?" Walker looked as though he would laugh. "From Colonials? I vow you could not under-stand the concept, let alone practice it."

"We understand it well enough to want to save a shipmate's life," Fane said, and thought for a moment that he had allowed a dangerous contempt to creep into his tone. Captain Walker's nostrils flared, and he began to lower the hand that had restrained his men from throwing Powell overboard.

"We will swear to call no man 'captain' but you," Fane said rapidly. "We will swear to work your ship as well as we would our own."

"You will do that anyway, whether or not you swear it," Walker said, amused. "The lash can see to that." He put his hand to his chin, his eyes brightening with interest. "But how can you make these promises for the others, bumpkin?" He raised a gloved finger to flick the lapel of Fane's coat. "You are no sailor. What position did you hold on the ship?"

"I was only a passenger," Fane answered truthfully. "A merchant, returning home."

"Ah," Walker said, glancing over at the other ship, where a number of his crew were busy loading choice contents from the hold into longboats. "Then that was your cloth we claim for the King?"

"My coffee and tea and spices," Fane corrected him, his jaw tight.

"So I ask you again—how can you promise anything in the name of these men?" Walker asked, but he had already focused more of his attention on the angle of the sun in the sky than on their discussion.

"I cannot. But you can ask them yourself, sir," Fane tried not to spit out the word, "and by extracting their promise, save another man for the King's navy."

Walker glanced back at Fane, then down the line of men, now divided in two by Powell's removal from their number. Captain Walker lifted his hand in a questioning gesture. "What say you? Would you save this man Powell by giving your word to be obedient and diligent in your duties?''

There were glowers and dark looks, but every head nodded. It was an easy enough promise to make, after all, for Walker was entirely correct: they would comply, promises or no promises, or else feel the lash's sting. Once free of their bonds, the only escape open to them would be the sea—and the open ocean was no escape, not even for those who could swim.

Walker lifted an imperious eyebrow, but then he made a gesture of clemency. Powell was dropped unceremoniously to the deck.

"There now! We have an understanding." He started to turn away, but then turned back, his forefinger lifted as if he had just had a thought. "Oh, but there is one other thing you will all do as well."

Every man stared, and even the normally staunch Powell did not raise his voice to ask what this one more condition would be.

"I will not have schemes of mutiny hatched upon my ship, gentlemen. Therefore I insist that no crewman will speak, ever, to this man Powell. Nor will Powell speak to any of you." He pointed casually toward the vanquished captain, whose fists were still caught beneath his chin as he had struggled to sit up on the deck.

The finger shifted to Fane. "Your name, bumpkin?"

"Peter White," Fane said, tensing.

"Nor will you speak, ever, to White. Nor will you write notes nor receive notes from either man. They will speak only when I or one of my officers have given them direct instructions to do so."

Fane glared at the British captain, but the man's

logic was inescapable. He saw both Powell and Fane as leaders, the kind of men to stir up trouble, even rebellion, and Fane had only his own actions to blame for that conclusion. He could not regret it, though, not if it had bought Powell's life. They had sailed together on at least half a dozen runs, and while he would not call Powell his friend, he respected the man's abilities and fairness.

"The penalty, gentlemen, if you are caught breaking this condition will be ten lashes." Walker frowned and shook his head. "No, I amend that. The penalty will be ten lashes—and then you will be cast into the sea. Do we understand one another?"

There were a few cautious nods, but mostly the men did not even dare to meet the captain's eyes.

"It seems we do," Walker said with seeming cheerfulness. "Now, Lieutenant Ames here will dole out your assignments for the next shift. Anyone not complying completely with his orders will be shot at once."

With that, Walker pivoted with military precision, and moved to return to his quarters.

The newly impressed men had grumbled among themselves as they were one by one untied from the nooselike ropes. Not one of them, Fane had noted with a sinking sense of despair at this sign of what his future held, dared to look at either him or Powell when they spoke.

Twelve

There were more, darker memories of Walker, and of the odious secret they both carried, but the memories raced from Fane's mind as he looked across the Mullitons' drawingroom, his gaze locking with that of Walker.

Walker could not hide the shock that seized him, not for the length of two whole heartbeats, but then a calm, almost serene mask slid over his features. Fane had seen that mask in place before, and was not fooled into thinking the man was either calm or serene. It must be just like looking at a ghost, for Walker would have long since hoped that Fane was dead.

Had Fane looked so pale as Walker now did, when he had seen the man in naval uniform who had come to his father's funeral? Fane was glad he had been spared that, at least, glad there had been no disastrous confrontation over his father's casket.

"Come and meet the new Lord Galbreth," he clearly heard Mrs. Mulliton tell the late arrival, and Fane realized there was no point in trying to avoid coming face-to-face with Walker. Once recognition had flared, a meeting was inevitable.

Fane glanced at Miss Hampton, tempted to tell her she must leave, at once, before the scene became ugly . . . but she was not looking at him. She was smiling in greeting at Walker. Too late, too late for her to be left out of the unpleasantness, Fane thought with a sinking heart.

Mrs. Mulliton and Walker stopped before them, but the man did not look to Fane. First he inclined his head in a half-bow to Miss Hampton, who curtsied in return. "Miss Hampton," he greeted her. "You appear to advantage tonight."

"Thank you, Mr. Walker," Miss Hampton replied, and the pinkish tinge on her cheeks bloomed into a rose to match her pelisse.

"Mister" Walker? Fane thought. The man certainly did not wear his regimentals, dressed tonight in much the same apparel as every other man in the room, with the exception of Rector Manning who was all in his parochial black. Had Walker left the navy—or had his sins finally been uncovered, and the man cast out?

"How is your aunt?" Walker inquired of Miss Hampton, his voice smooth as silk as he still avoided turning to Fane.

"Very well, thank you. She is here tonight."

"Then I will have to seek her out. I am only sorry that she was with friends when I came by yesterday."

Came by? Fane remembered the laughter he had heard when Miss Hampton had met up with a mounted man yesterday. There was every possibility that man had been Walker. The thought of the malicious former captain accompanying Miss Hampton to a house from which her aunt was absent made Fane narrow his eyes.

As if sensing the ill will emanating from Fane,

Walker turned to him at last. There was a secondary shock as their gazes locked once more.

"Lord Galbreth, please allow me to introduce Mr. Walker," Mrs. Mulliton said with a bright smile. "He is new to our little district, not unlike Miss Hampton, and yourself of course!" Belatedly she added the introduction in reverse, "Mr. Walker, please meet Lord Galbreth."

He was holding his breath, Fane realized, awaiting the moment Walker revealed that they had met before, that both of them had borne different titles then. Exclamations of surprise would surround them, and then a flood of questions. So much for an existence in England, Fane thought with a harsh twist of his lips. He would have to return to America . . . if he could, if he was not arrested before he could buy passage on a ship.

"Lord Galbreth," Walker said, and bowed from the waist.

Fane stared, distantly aware he must bow in return, that his lack was creating a stir among the observers— but what was this? Walker did not denounce him, did not call him by the name of Peter White, had not stated that the Watch should be called in to arrest the deserter among them.

Walker straightened, and in an instant Fane understood. It was all there in Walker's half-lidded eyes, in the way he seemed poised to take a blow: Walker desperately wanted to keep his own secret.

If the man dared to proclaim the truth about Fane, he risked having his own true nature revealed. To denounce Fane might well destroy the fabric of Walker's existence—an existence presumably already

tattered around its edges. Mrs. Mulliton had not said
that Walker was visiting, rather that he had been *living* here for three months; the man was hiding in
the most rural hamlet his twisted soul could bear.
Once this withdrawal was no longer a haven for him,
where could he retreat to then?

"Pardon me," Fane heard his own voice speaking,
as some instinct took over to fill the awkward moment. "I am more accustomed to shaking hands than
to bowing," he gave the lame justification. People
might not believe the words, for Fane had been bowing to acquaintances all night, but some excuse was
needed to smooth over his lapse in expected manners. Fane bowed his head to Walker, but he was
unable to give the man any higher salute than that,
not even in the name of maintaining the civility of
his hostess's assembly.

"No apology needed, Lord Galbreth," Walker said
with the barest hint of a smile and ever so slight a
hesitation over the name.

"Do you go to Mrs. Auden's musicale tomorrow evening?" Miss Hampton asked Walker, saving Fane from
having to make a reply.

Walker gave a nod as he answered yes, and the conversation fell to commonalties. Fane scarcely partici-
pated, on the one hand knowing too few of the names
and events mentioned, and on the other instead
choosing to stand back mentally, watching Walker's
every move, every expression.

Mr. Walker must have been the final expected guest,
for after a minute Mrs. Mulliton announced that it
was now time to form tables for whist. It was with a
sense of relief that Fane learned he was not to be at

Walker's table—but, he noted with a scowl, Miss Hampton was.

If he'd doubted before that Walker was the man the village called Miss Hampton's beau, Fane doubted it no longer. Not only had their hostess seated the two as partners, but Fane's own table mates shared similar confirmations with him in the course of conversation over their cardplay. He learned that Miss Hampton and Mr. Walker "made a handsome couple when they danced," and that they were "seen in close conversation at chapel last Sunday," and that "Mr. Walker has said to Mr. Beauthorpe that he means to settle down and marry."

Walker? Marry? Fane lifted his gaze from his cards to glare at the other man, the man who had once held Fane captive on his ship. He played his cards reflexively, and he remembered. . . .

Fane had been standing at the prow of the *HMS Valiton*, peeling apples at the rail and letting the peels fall into the ocean. The night was calm, so Cook had decided to stew some of the more withered apples against the chance that tomorrow would not provide the kind of weather in which he could have a fire aboard. Fane had raised his hand to volunteer for peeling duty. It gave him a reason to be above deck. It was not Fane's scheduled shift; he ought to be sleeping while the opportunity was there—but he knew he would not be able to easily find rest.

The night air seemed to be thickening, the light grey mist hinting at a thicker fog to come. That was all to the good, and Fane could be excused for won-

dering if the weather reached out to lend a helping
hand.

Fane glanced to where a light flickered on the distant shore—someone must have a bonfire burning.
Smugglers perhaps, signaling to their collaborators.
Was that Virginia? Or Georgia? He had lost track of
the changes in the ship's course. It was Walker's way
to counsel with his ranking officers privately, and it
was everyone else's duty to jump to when told and
never mind the fine points such as revealing a destination.

They traveled mostly by night, like thieves, and such
they were for Walker had let it be known that he would
not sail for England until he could present his supe-
riors with the finest, the best, and the most. It was not
enough that the captain would be praised for the quality merchandise he had commandeered from the two
ships his men had boarded; it was not enough that he
had sunk the enemy ships that they might not be recovered and used again against the British force—no,
Captain Walker also wanted his record, upon returning, to show the highest number of men pressed into
His Majesty's service.

They would have to raid another ship of its cache
of food to even have a hope of making the journey to
England—and with another supposed twenty or thirty
men aboard, the weeks of open sea voyaging would
be lean and hungry ones all the same. Fane had no
doubt he and the other "new" men would be chained
in the hold once a likely ship was targeted. They would
wait with shackles on their wrists to see if Walker could
conquer yet another ship . . . or whether their own

ship would be vanquished. If it were sunk, and the shackles still hung heavy on their wrists . . .

Fane took several deep breaths, to quiet his indignation before it could boil out of his mouth in the form of spoken curses. He'd gone three weeks without speaking scarcely a word, except those ordered from him by Walker or Lieutenant Ames. Better not to allow the indignities to sap his control . . . except control was only possible because little Ollie crouched nearby, trying to be invisible behind a coil of thick rope.

The poor lad did not quake or moan—he was too afraid to risk making any sound and thereby be discovered on the deck after dark had fallen. Too soon he would be called back to his new duties as cabin boy to his captor. Too soon he would sport another blackened eye or red welt. Too soon . . . worse would happen. Fane clenched his fist, almost unable to contemplate what "worse" was, except that Ollie's whispered words rang through his head, over and over again.

Ollie knew Fane could not tell what he heard, not unless Fane wished to risk the lash and then drowning. That was no doubt why the lad dared to say anything aloud at all. Ollie faced the same punishment himself. The boy's very real peril made his whimpered confessions that much more believable, more real, more horrible.

"He touches me," Ollie had confessed within a week of their capture. "The captain. I'm desperate afeared he means to . . ."

Words had failed him then as silent tears took over, but Fane had not required a term for the blood to chase out of his head in appalled outrage. The allegation was almost too loathsome to grasp, but it only took a few dangerous, quick words between them for Fane to be convinced the boy understood well enough what manner of threat Walker posed to him—and Fane had no doubt the offenses would only worsen with time.

The worst of it was that Fane had no authority, no power to protect the lad. The best he could do was to go and stand before Ames silently until the lieutenant gave him permission to speak. Then Fane would request that Ollie be assigned to some night duty or other—night being the time he was most likely to be at Walker's mercy. Fane pretended he needed the help, or that Ollie had misbehaved and the extra work was to serve as punishment. Sometimes Ames agreed. Fane could not be sure if the man suspected what Fane knew about their captain, and he dare not ask what had happened to the prior cabin boy. He dare not risk offending the one man who took some mercy, wittingly or otherwise, on the lad.

"Boy!" came the cry, ripping the night's peace, causing Fane to startle, losing a whole apple overboard. It was Davidson, looking for the lad, no doubt ordered to do so by Captain Walker. "Boy" was Walker's only name for Ollie, and the crew had taken up the practice.

"Boy!" Davidson, his beefy neck too thick to allow him to button the topmost button of his uniform coat, pointed at Fane. "Where's the boy?"

Fane shook his head and tapped his lips with a knuckle, the sign he had taken up to remind others of the prohibition the captain had put on him. Davidson, even though he had obviously been at his daily ration of rum, remembered at once. "That's right! No talkin' fer you," Davidson said in a mocking tone. "But you can point right enough, so I'll have an answer out of you. You seen the boy?"

Fane shook his head, trying to look as indifferent as possible.

Davidson growled, but he turned and rocked away down the deck, calling again, "Boy!"

"I'll be worse beat fer this when I'm found," Ollie's unsteady whisper came, filled with dread. "I don't know as what's worse—when th' captain's mad at me, or when he pretends he likes me."

Fane winced, only belatedly thinking to loosen his grip on the paring knife in his hand when its edge threatened to bite into his finger. If only it weren't a small, virtually useless blade, if only he had a cutlass or one of the military swords Walker had mounted on the wall of his cabin. "I will see the man is reported for this," Fane said in a hot whisper. "He will lose his colors. This is unconscionable—"

"Shhh!" Ollie hissed. "Don't talk! Don't get killed, Mr. White!"

Fane bit his tongue, hoping his silence would serve to chase the note of hysteria from the lad's speech.

"Boy!" distantly came Davidson's bellow from the other end of the deck. There was a curse, broken by the wind, and then Fane heard the last bit of a question Davidson had called out: "—there in the crow's nest! D'you see the boy?"

There were three long seconds of silence, then a return call that Fane could not make out over the slap of water against the prow.

It was Ollie's involuntary whimper that confirmed

Davidson strode back their way. Fane did not turn to the sailor, acting as if he had no knowledge of anything, hoping that by some luck the lad would yet be overlooked.

Davidson killed that hope in a moment when he stepped around the coil of rope and roughly pulled Ollie from where he had crouched. He held the boy fast by the ear. "If'n the captain didn't want you quick like, boy, I'd be powerful tempted to teach you to hide from me."

"I weren't hiding," Ollie squeaked, the lie as obvious from his tone as from his shaking limbs.

"Get on with you!" Davidson growled as he thrust Ollie toward the ship's cabins. He took a swing with his foot at Ollie's backside, which missed, causing Davidson to nearly lose his footing before he regained his balance and stumbled away, in Ollie's wake.

Fane gritted his teeth so hard his jaw ached. The peels his shaking hands took off the next apple were so thick as to scarcely leave any of the fruit behind. With a curse he could not quite keep under his breath, Fane threw the fruit in the basket at his feet, and plunged the paring knife into the ship's rail, not caring of any lashes he might have to take for damaging the ship. He breathed deeply, leaning his hands on the rail as he rocked in place, fighting to master his helpless fury.

It was too much for a man to bear, this ship and its tyrant captain.

It was too much that the normally gregarious Powell slipped each day into a darker despair, the former captain locked in a voiceless isolation as complete as Fane's own.

It was too much that Walker would call Fane into his cabin, where he would fire insult after insult at Fane, condemning all things American, accusing all "Colonists" of being traitors. He said "these rebels" were idiots and cretins and worse—and all the time Fane could do nothing but stand there, ordered into silence, knowing the man who taunted him, who dared him to speak so that he might punish Fane for it, was no better than the names he called his captives.

It was too much that in three weeks' time Walker had ordered half a dozen men flogged—the last one for no greater offense than a look the captain claimed Edwards had given him. A *look!*

It was all too much, too unfair, too deliberately severe—but the worst of it all was what Ollie must endure.

Fane hauled up the basket of peeled apples, leaving the unpeeled ones scattered behind on the deck. He'd get them later. For now he needed to move. He couldn't stand still, not while his imagination ran rampant. . . .

From inside the nearest cabin a shrill scream filled the night, hanging heavy on the thick, damp air. A soul-deep chill chased through Fane, but a moment later he dropped the basket as a white-hot rage filled him.

Without clear thought, he strode forward, putting out a hand to shove aside a uniformed sailor who stood guard at the cabin door belonging to Captain Walker. The guard shouted in surprise, and recovered his balance, turning with readied fists to challenge Fane, but by then Fane already had the cabin door open.

He froze, not quite sure what to make of the scene

before him. A wild-eyed Ollie cowered in the corner
of the bunk, his hands lashed together before him,
Walker leaning over him with one knee on the bunk.
When a coatless Walker spun to face him, Fane saw
that Walker's hands were filled with fabric—a cloth to
stuff in the mouth, another to tie it in place. Ollie was
barechested, his shirt tossed to one side of the room,
and one side of Ollie's face was bright red, as if he
had been slapped.

"Damn it, get out of here!" Walker bellowed. He
moved swiftly, planting his hand on Fane's chest, shov-
ing him back. "Jenkins! Get this stupid fool out of
here and chain him in the hold."

The guard, Jenkins, stumbled back as Fane was
pushed into him, and nearly fell.

"At once!" Walker shouted, his eyes showing white.

The guard's imbalance lasted a moment too long,
however, for Fane leaped back into the room, and
reached for the nearest sword. He pulled it from the
scabbard in which it hung suspended, the blade making a faint metallic woosh as it pulled clear. He swung
the blade around, leveling it at Walker's chest. "I will
be damned before I will let you harm this lad again,"
Fane vowed.

Walker's upper lip curled in disdain. "You will certainly be damned." He gave a sideways glance at the
guard. "Jenkins, call more men! We'll put this blackguard overboard without going to the trouble of flog-
ging him first."

Jenkins backed away, shouting for assistance and
earning a dark look from his captain, presumably for
leaving Walker alone with an armed man. "Imbecile!"
Walker spat after the man.

Fane stood poised, the tip of the sword pressing into Walker's shirtfront. It would only take a moment for the man to be dead. That would be Fane's compensation while he himself drowned in the sea.

"I would spare your life, if only I could extract a believable promise from you that you would leave the boy alone," Fane told the captain.

Walker's eyes burned with fury and his fists clenched, but Fane could also see that the man dare not move, not with the thick metal blade pressing against his breastbone.

Fane pulled the blade back, prepared to thrust, and Walker took a step back and threw up his arms as if they could possibly protect him, when a blur of motion came between them. "Ollie!" Fane shouted, but the boy was already out the cabin door. With a wild scream, the lad threw himself over the ship's rail, his still bound hands cradled before him. A moment later there was the inevitable splash, cutting off the tail end of the boy's cry.

Fane charged in Ollie's wake, coming up hard against the rail, but the night had already swallowed any sign of the lad.

The sound of running feet announced the arrival of a half dozen men, who converged on Fane. They crowded around him, just out of the immediate reach of the sword. Over their shoulders Fane could see the troubled faces of some of the American crew, and with the kind of idle clarity that comes with the knowledge of inescapable disaster, he wondered if the men might take this chance to stage a revolt. It would, unfortunately, end in their slaughter, for Walker's men were armed, and Walker would want nothing less than the destruction of any man who acted against him. He might even forget his desire to bring a multitude of pressed men to England and order them all killed.

It only took a moment for Fane to decide what he must do. He must not be the cause of all these good men's deaths. He must not allow Walker's men to seize him, to bind his hands and feet. Instead he followed in the brave young Ollie's footsteps, and leaned far back, rolling over the rail until the terror of falling was abruptly ended by the dark, cold waters of the Atlantic Ocean as it swallowed him up.

The memories were foggy and unclear from there. Fane remembered calling out Ollie's name, and trying to swim toward the area he thought the boy might be. He remembered sudden waves that filled his nose and mouth with water, and he remembered being lifted by the waves enough that every once and a while he could see the bonfire burning on that far distant shore—an impossible goal, for very shortly the viciously cold water had chilled him, and made his limbs heavy and his brain numb.

He had no memory of the smugglers' longboat, nor of being plucked from the sea by its men, not until he awoke blindfolded near an extinguished fire, with a goose egg sized bump on his head. They let him have warmed grog, no doubt made from French spirits smuggled onto American soil—and let him sit until he was able to stand. He asked if they had found the boy, but their only answer was that no one had known to look for a boy—they had found Fane only because their longboat had collided with him in the dark.

"You saved us dear, you did," an unseen smuggler told him with a gruff voice tinged by approval.

Fane was not so far out of his head as to think that approval would include allowing him to remove the blindfold, so he left it where it was tied, speaking to the disembodied voices around him. "You were making a run tonight."

"We'd no idea there was an enemy ship in the bay," came the affirmation. "If our delivery men'd come along just then, we'd'a been out all those supplies and a ship too! We think th' ship what dropped you overboard was one under a man named Walker—"

"It was. I was impressed into his crew," Fane said.

He heard the smuggler spit in disgust. "Thieving bastard! Well, then I say to you, best watch your backside, and choose a life other than the sea! If'n you ever encounter Walker again, he'll see you hanged from the yardarm, and no second thoughts about it neither."

"He'll think I have drowned."

"Not 'til he sees your bloated body, he won't. No, that one will have you listed as a deserter, and there'll be a warrant out against you. To the Brits you'll be a wanted man, mark my words."

Fane could not argue. He had exposed Walker's dark secret, and even if Jenkins had been too thick to realize what was happening in that cabin, having even one man possibly still alive who knew the truth would be enough to fan the flame of Walker's fury, to make the captain dread the remote possibility that Fane was not dead.

One of their number led Fane from the spot, yet blindfolded, and put him on a cart with a driver. The driver drove him to the nearest town—Little Creek, Delaware—and left him at its border, requesting that

Fane leave the blindfold in place until the cart had retreated.

He complied out of gratitude for his rescue, and could not resent that the smuggler left him at the edge of the woods with no money and certainly no papers. Too, he was yet soaked to the skin, and smelling of liquor—but Fane's newest despair was short-lived, because he quickly realized there was bound to be at least one captain in the port on the other side of town, one who could vouch for him, and even take him up as a passenger.

He was home in Philadelphia within two days, his bump already receding but his heart heavy at the loss of the brave little lad, Ollie, and the fears he had for the men yet held under Walker's tyranny. The joy on his mother's face, however, helped to relieve his sorrow, and he was warmly greeted by his employers, who along with Mama had feared the worst once word of the American ship Walker had destroyed had been carried back to shore some three weeks past.

Fane had claimed the escape had injured his back, making it impossible for him to sail anymore, and his duties had shifted over to helping manage the coffee-house and the flow of its supplies from the warehouses. It was not the life he would have preferred, but he'd decided he could not put his mother through another terror such as she had known—and he could not risk recapture by the English, for that would have been a death sentence.

And now, a year later, after the war was over, now that the English had agreed in principle and in practice to no longer impress even British-born sailors from American ships, now Fane knew there was only one man who might still want to link the names of Peter White and Fane Westby—the man across the room who smiled and chatted over cards with Miss Hampton.

Thirteen

Why ever is Lord Galbreth so distracted tonight? Marietta thought as she laid down a playing card. He was staring intensely one moment, and the next his vision was turned inward, to judge by the vague frown fixed on his features. Had he received unfavorable word from the solicitors, and so soon?

"Bah!" cried Marietta's partner, Mr. Walker, as he sat back in his chair. "They have defeated us entirely, Miss Hampton," he said of the other pair of cardplayers. Theirs was the last table to finish play, all other contests having already been decided, the guests rising to partake of the wine and cakes that had been set out for them to enjoy.

"I am afraid we did not have the luck tonight," Marietta conceded. She did not add that she may have been distracted by Lord Galbreth's peculiar behavior. A tinge of guilt struck her, for she had not served as much of a tutor to him tonight.

She rose from her chair, murmuring her pardons for moving away. Mr. Walker stood as if he would accompany her, but Marietta turned quickly, pretending she had not noted his intention.

She wandered toward a table laden with glasses of wine, but her real intent was not to secure the drink but rather to move closer to where Lord Galbreth stood talking with Mr. Mulliton.

"I understand Galbreth had the rectory's door replaced," Sir Eustace was saying to Miss Prentice as Marietta strolled by, her steps slowing as she heard the name. "Rector Manning is best pleased to be able to use his front door again."

"And I have it from my maid that the Widow Gilley's boy is more than contented as a stable lad for Westby Hall. His hiring will mean all the difference for them come winter."

"Too unlucky a thing that Gilley's horse bolted. . . ."

Marietta moved on, now the conversation had turned to old news of Mr. Gilley's unfortunate death. She now carried a wineglass in hand, even though she did not have much of a head for wine. But a glass was almost as convenient a prop as a fan. *And why am I in need of a prop?* she asked herself. Because a prop was easy to hide behind, and wine could be used to explain away a flushed complexion. *And why would I be blushing?*

Almost against her will, her gaze shifted, seeking out the tall figure of Lord Galbreth. He was the reason she would blush, of course. Just to be in the same room with him was to be affected by his presence, his size and stature. It was to remember any kindness extended . . . and to recall the way he had touched her face.

Her gaze slid to observe Mr. Walker. He, too, had touched her chin some weeks ago, and she had liked him a little better for it at the time . . . but the simple truth was the memory of it was just a memory, not a tingling reality that disordered her thoughts at the strangest moments as this other memory did. Disordered thoughts indeed! That was what she experienced even now as she glanced from under her lashes once more at Lord Galbreth.

The problem with Galbreth was that he made all other men in the room pale in comparison. It was not just his size, either. As commanding a presence as he possessed, it was the intelligence in his face, the unexpected touches of compassion that secured Marietta's focus on him.

She'd had every reason to fear the worst from him, and had given him every chance to know the worst of her. Her inappropriately frivolous clothing told the tale of how she'd come down in the world, for the silks and satins were befitting a London drawingroom, and were clearly all wrong for walking about the countryside and picking quantities of wildflowers. If Galbreth had missed the telling details of her clothing, there was her own stubbornly forthright comments and actions to tell him she was no proper lady. She carried a pistol about, engaged in trade, haggled for money, and haggled with *him* for the right to stay in the dower house. Oh yes, it had to be abundantly clear to Lord Galbreth that his tenant was no gentlewoman, not anymore.

The truth was, it was difficult to appear so much at disadvantage before the man. His behavior had convinced her he was a good man, a worthy man to follow in his father's footsteps as master of the manor, a natural leader who also understood the quality of mercy. She had not needed to overhear the favorable comments made about Galbreth by others to know his value for herself.

Marietta admitted, with something very close to an ache in her chest, that she wished to be admired by him—or she would even settle for being *liked* by him. She wanted to remain in the dower house, but the wanting to be there went deeper than it had before, was born of more than the simple desire to keep a roof over her head. She wanted time for some finer emotion to develop between herself and Galbreth: friendship, or barring that, at least respect. But how could he possibly respect her? Everything she did, every action she took, declared her a hoyden. She had held her chin high among the villagers of Kendall Town these three months past, had even been accepted into their fold, bless them, but she found now that this one man's acceptance meant more to her than all the others' combined.

So how to win such a man's respect? Simple: become respectable. And what one way was there for a woman to be respectable—at least as Society saw the word? Why, to marry of course.

Marietta's gaze slid to where Mr. Walker was obtaining a glass of wine. Here was a man who might consider marrying her. She and Mr. Walker certainly had the most in common: both had been banished from the life they had known. There was one difference, though. Marietta longed for the privileges she had lost, but she was not so sure she missed the life she had led beyond the comforts those privileges could buy her; whereas Mr. Walker could not hide that he felt this life in Kendall Town was beneath him, that along with privilege he had lost his contentment.

There was a restlessness in him—but perhaps that was why he courted Marietta, albeit in his half-hearted manner.

Perhaps he sought her out because she could understand his loss. Perhaps he hoped a wife, and eventually children, would fill the void left behind when he had been forced from the navy. She knew he lived from the income from investments, and that he had some quarterly family money that came in, but perhaps he would be more content were he to find a new vocation. It was difficult to imagine Mr. Walker as a farmer, but even in Kendall Town there were surely other tasks at which he could lay his hands?

It was then that she saw Lord Galbreth had moved, that he now approached Mr. Walker. She could not hear their words, but the sweeping gesture Galbreth executed made it obvious he was inviting Mr. Walker to join him. The two turned together, striding with purpose out the single open door that led to Mrs. Mulliton's small garden. Marietta glanced about, realizing that no one else had noted the interchange. As casually as she could, she followed the gentlemen out the door.

She got no more then two feet out the door before she saw the men were at the other side of the vegetable patch that the Mulliton's grew just beyond a more decorative flower patch. Marietta supposed with growing perplexity that the two men had most likely moved out, risking mud on their bootheels, because they chose not to be overheard. There was no way to come closer to the men without making her presence obvious, so Marietta froze where she was.

Despite their caution, the wind carried some of their words to her ears.

". . . will say nothing . . . !" came Mr. Walker's voice, the words hotly couched.

"Only one thing keeps me silent—" The wind snatched away the rest of Galbreth's reply.

". . . Miss Hampton!" partially came Walker's reply. Marietta flushed scarlet to hear they spoke of her, but not completely because of embarrassment. It was . . . gratifying, yes, admit it, to know that her name, her being, had something to do with the agitation between the two men. She had seen the like before, in London: two young bucks vying to see who would capture some beautiful young woman's approval. They had circled and all but spat like cats, and the young woman's estimation had been enhanced by their silly display. Not that Marietta believed for a moment that *she* was the source of some romantic friction between these two men, but it seemed clear that Lord Galbreth was trying to warn Mr. Walker away, and that thought filled her with a totally inappropriate warmth.

And Mr. Walker was resisting, vehemently.

She could see, as Mr. Walker turned away angrily from Galbreth, that only then did he become aware that Marietta had been observing them. He hesitated, perhaps wondering how much Marietta could have heard, but a heartbeat later he strode determinedly toward her.

"The buffoon," he said in a very low voice she just barely caught as he approached, and she doubted she was meant to hear the words. There was a strange kind of glitter in Mr. Walker's eyes—she might even call it triumphant.

Marietta glanced toward the garden, seeing Lord Galbreth standing, his shoulders rigid, his vision cast to the ground as though he struggled to master some emotion. She took half a step in his direction, but Mr. Walker's hand came up and caught her elbow.

Marietta turned back to Mr. Walker. "It is obvious you two know each other," she stated.

"Yes," Mr. Walker answered, his jaw working for a moment. "Or rather," he said, sliding her a sideward look, "he knows *of* me. It would seem Lord Galbreth has acquaintances in London, acquaintances who have carried false tales to his ears. I have told you how it is that I was forced from the navy by specious and false lies told of me. Galbreth chooses to believe those lies, to condemn me on sight."

"On sight?" Marietta questioned with a frown. "How can he know you on sight?"

"I misspoke, dear lady. Of course I meant he was prepared to dislike me from the very moment he heard my name."

Marietta's brow cleared, but she frowned again a moment later. "That seems very unlike Lord Galbreth—"

"Just as those lies are very unlike the truth in my case, Miss Hampton! I beg you to keep in mind how long you have had to judge my nature, against how long you have had to judge Galbreth's. He is surely, at the very least, a fortune-hunter, you must admit. For why else did he never call upon his father until the man lay at death's door?"

"I do not know," Marietta admitted slowly. How long had Lord Galbreth known about his father? Could he have come earlier?

Mr. Walker's eyes darkened. "And, as much as it hurts me to do so, my dear, dear lady, I must tell you," he caught up her hand, "that Galbreth has heard whispers of your own indiscretion."

Marietta blanched, as Mr. Walker stared at her intently, as if he could read her thoughts through her face. Was that a grimace that curved his lips—it could not be a slight smile, could it?

"He said some rather unkind things about you. He warned me to stay clear of you, that you had been known to have your run of the fields and to carry a pistol about with you. He warned me it is said that you are most dangerous with a pistol in hand—Miss Hampton, my heart! You look as though you might faint! Here, take my hand and sit here a spell. . . ."

He helped her to a chair, and rambled on with concerned, soft, inquiring comments, but they made little sense past the ringing in Marietta's ears. It was as bad as she had feared, as unkind a reality as she had wished away: Lord Galbreth not only did not like her, he had so little respect for her that he was willing to vilify her behind her back.

I must move as soon as may be! her mind cried, and she could have wept at the immediate denial of the possibility of moving. Trapped, she was trapped, even more than when she had feared what gossip might do to the shreds of her reputation. At least then she'd had a choice—but now! Now even though she could not bear to stay, she could not afford to go.

A shadow crossed between her and the room's center, and Marietta looked up to find Lord Galbreth standing before her. Mr. Walker released her hand and stood up straight, glaring at Galbreth.

"Miss Hampton," Galbreth said, his look troubled. "I am . . . I wish to know if you still mean to attend Mrs. Auden's musicale tomorrow?"

Marietta just stared up at him, unable to speak for expecting his next words, the words that invited her *not* to approach him, *not* to serve as tutor any longer to him.

He stared, awaiting a reply. Mr. Walker leaned down and whispered in Marietta's ear. "It is all right, my dear. I shall go, too."

Marietta looked from one man to the other, feeling stupid and thick. Belatedly she nodded in reply to Galbreth's question.

Galbreth lids half-lowered over his eyes, but it was not a malicious look that hid behind the screen of lashes. What was it then? Doubt? Disgust? Or something else?

"Then may I bring around my coach to take you and your aunt up tomorrow evening at seven?" Galbreth asked.

Marietta's thoughts spun even more than they had before, for the request utterly baffled her. Where was his rejection, his rebuff of her company?

"The lady has already granted me that privilege," Mr. Walker answered in her place. Marietta nodded once, stiffly, seizing on the lie as a refuge, a place to hide until she could find a way to understand why Galbreth not only did not denounce her, but sought to maintain some affected pretense of approval of her.

Aunt Silvia floated into Marietta's field of vision, and the look on her aunt's face grew alarmed. "Why, Marietta!" she cried, "you are pale as a ghost!" She put out a hand to press it to Marietta's cheek. "And a little warm, too. Do you wish to leave? I think we should return home."

"Oh yes, please," Marietta said, and had never wanted anything so much in her life, not even a reprieve from her papa's final disapproval. She could bear being rejected by Lord Galbreth, if only he would do so, cleanly, clearly, all at once—but she could not fathom why he looked down on her with troubled eyes that told her nothing of his thoughts, his real opinions. She could not bear knowing what Mr. Walker had told her, and yet being unable to see that reality in Galbreth's gaze, of daring to hope for one fluttering heartbeat that Mr. Walker had been mistaken. . . .

As Aunt Silvia and Mr. Walker led her toward the front door, calling for the gig and for their wraps, Marietta cast one last glance back at Lord Galbreth. She did not seek approbation or acquittal, but she dared to hope she might see the barest flicker of regret.

Marietta saw none of those things, but what she saw shocked her to her very core: she was no expert at deciphering others' emotions, but upon the Holy Book she would swear it was anguish she saw writ large across Lord Galbreth's features.

Miss Hampton avoided Fane as assiduously as a fox avoided the pack of baying hounds pursuing it. If Fane sat in the far left seat of the first row of chairs at Mrs. Auden's musicale, Miss Hampton sat in the far right seat of the third row. If he crossed to refill his goblet with wine from the serving tray near where she stood, Miss Hampton fled to examine the music mounted before one of the hired musicians. If he sauntered toward the group wherein she chatted, she excused herself and moved to another.

There was no doubt that Mr. Walker had poisoned her mind against Fane.

Curious how deeply her renunciation stabbed Fane . . . but not so curious, really. It hurt to know that whatever Walker had said, Miss Hampton had believed it. He was not sure why she was so willing to accept the worst about him, but clearly she had.

The normal response, he thought to himself with a bitter smile, would be to respond in kind, to find the faults in Miss Hampton. How was it then that Fane found his attention focused on Miss Hampton, yes, but not to find blame or fault, but rather the opposite? There were prettier women in the room, make no mistake, but the lovely Miss Harding was too often cool and cutting in her ways, and the dimple-cheeked Miss Dampshire was always flighty and incapable of serious thought. Mrs. Plower was striking, but she lacked a certain carriage, a certain dash that Miss Hampton conveyed with nothing more than that marvelous smile of hers. Miss Hampton's unusual good looks drew the eye for a re-evaluation in a way a more noticeably pretty face would not. Her laugh was a delight, and even though her features were today haunted by whatever ghosts Walker had seen fit to raise, there was a discernment in her gaze that drew others to her. She knew the tricks of keeping a conversation going, of making the other party feel engaged and involved . . . and Fane knew a breath-stealing sense of loss that she no longer turned her charms to work on him.

Walker was by her side every moment. This came

as no surprise to Fane. Walker had warned him away from Miss Hampton . . . Marietta. He would not call her thus by her Christian name, not aloud, especially not now that he had slipped so far in her regard . . . but in his thoughts she had become "Marietta" to him. The name suited her—a little exotic, attractive, charming. Perhaps it was the influence of the music washing all around them, played by the musicians Mrs. Auden had hired, but it seemed of a sudden to him that there was a musical quality to that name, Marietta.

He would have to talk to her, have to get her to confess what Walker had told her, so that he might have the chance to correct the whispers with which Walker had filled Marietta's ears. There was a danger in that plan, of course. Walker had made it very clear that if Fane told anyone, most especially Marietta, what Fane had seen that day in the captain's cabin, what he presumed must have led one way or the other to Walker's fall from grace, Walker would reveal that Fane was a deserter. One grievous wound would be exchanged for another—making it impossible for either man to remain in Kendall Town. Probably making it impossible for either to remain in England at all. Walker would not go down alone, he claimed— and Fane had every reason to believe him.

When had the man gained the upper hand, out there yesterday in Mrs. Mulliton's garden? At first, Fane had thought Walker had been cowed, but when they spoke more to the point, their voices rising despite their need for secrecy, somewhere along the line Walker had visibly puffed up, and somehow Fane had been the receiver of threats rather than the giver. Fane had said something . . . he could not think what. He'd only spoken the truth, only those facts Walker already knew. . . .

Now Walker had spread a set of lies before Marietta—something horrible, but also believable to her. Fane tossed down the last of the wine from his glass, and did not reach for another. Like his thoughts, the wine tasted bitter.

It was strange then, that in the musicians' interlude, everyone else seemed to take Fane in good regard. "I've a wish to try those rifles you've told Mr. Lumley you brought over the seas with you," Sir Eustace enthused at him. "Never fired an American-made weapon, I haven't! M'boy's traveled a bit though, you know, and he has nothing but praise for the American huntsman, and therefore their rifles. Can I talk you into a hunting party, and into bringing your rifles to it?"

Fane no sooner accepted that invitation than he was offered another by the elderly Mrs. Ratcliffe to come and tour her rose garden, to see if there were any American versions he knew of that she ought to have shipped over to enhance her lot.

Miss Partridge teased him gently, "My grandpapa tells me that America is filled with bears and wolves, that they wander the streets as freely as do the pigeons here."

Fane offered a lopsided smile, too keenly aware that he was the center of interest for everyone—everyone but Marietta. "Alas!" he said, perhaps too loudly, perhaps hoping that this interest in him by others would attract one particular lady's interest. "As a lad I could have only wished it were true! Bears and wolves would have been far more interesting than the watchmen and inebriates who patrolled the streets in their place. But do you know, Miss Partridge, that I find your streets, both here and in London, ever so much more fascinating than the ones in Philadelphia?"

"Indeed?" Miss Partridge looked pleased.

"Yes, indeed. Your city streets are often as not so ancient that they follow their own logic, twisting and wandering about from here to there, and creating fascinating little pigeonholes to explore. I am afraid that because the streets in Philadelphia are very clearly and logically laid out in a grid, they do not often lend themselves to making unexpected or interesting little corners and pockets in which to find adventure."

"In which to find pickpockets," drawled Toby Shreever, the lad rusticating from Oxford.

Everyone laughed, and then there was a sea of questions for Fane. What else was there to know about Philadelphia? That it was a lovely city, full of grand buildings, some of which could rival those of London.

Did they have opera there? Indeed, yes, and some of the best Italian opera to be heard.

What had surprised him most upon his arrival in England? That everywhere here he saw images of the King or the Crown, whereas in American it was the eagle that hung over every front door and shop.

It was all very pleasant, and he learned as much from his questioners as they perhaps learned from him . . . except for the one lady who did not approach, did not ask a question, did not even meet his eye. Marietta.

Marietta was busy elsewhere. Her hand was caught up in Walker's, as he leaned into her and spoke in urgent low tones to her alone. Once Marietta blushed

a deep, deep red, and her lips tightened, and Fane
would have pushed the sea of people aside, would have
crossed the room to smash Walker in the face with his
fist, except that only a few moments later Marietta
laughed. It was not a big laugh, and not especially
merry, but it froze Fane where he was, telling him that
whatever Walker had said it had not been an insult,
as Fane had imagined.

"Excuse me?" Fane murmured, forcing his attention back to Miss Partridge, who apparently was asking
him a question. Fane had not heard anything but an
inquiry in her voice, her words lost in his fervor to aid
Marietta . . . who, it seemed, was not the slightest bit
in need of his aid.

To speak or not to speak, *now* that *is the question*,
Fane thought sourly to himself. If he spoke, he must
leave England . . . and leave the matter of the dower
house to the unknown Cousin Malcolm in his stead.
What would this Malcolm do? Would he cast the ladies
out, regardless of their need? What would Marietta
do? But, perhaps more to the point, if Fane did not
speak against Walker, a far worse fate than simple poverty might be hers.

Somehow, he recalled again, as Walker and Fane
had stood confronting the past in the mud of Mrs.
Mulliton's garden, Walker had turned in a minute
from a sly-eyed scoundrel to a gleeful bully—his transformation making no sense to Fane, not then and not
now, in the light of another day. What had changed?
Why had Walker suddenly thought the scales had been
balanced between them? Whatever his reason,
Walker's next statement had been blunt enough: "I
mean to marry the girl."

"Why?" Fane had demanded, his heart sinking into the mud as surely as his bootheels had.

"Do not be purposefully dense," had been Walker's mean-spirited reply. "I must rebuild my reputation. No one will believe . . . those other accusations—"

"Truths. They were and remain truths," Fane had asserted. "What you meant to do to Ollie—! The beatings were nothing compared to your true intent. What happened to the other cabin boys you must have had over the years? Did they threaten to talk? Did you injure them too badly? Did you have to get rid of them? How often did a cabin boy go missing overboard? What was the matter? Could you not wait to put the gag in their mouths before you tried to—"

Walker cut him off with a vicious slash of his hand through the air, his nostrils dilating as if he barely contained his temper. "If I have a wife," Walker had said the words from between gritted teeth, "I will be seen to be leading the very manner of life that defies the kind of gossip that has dogged me since you cursedly came onto my ship."

"Were you at last caught *in flagrante delicto?*" Fane had pressed, knowing it must be so for the man to have left the navy. He would have had to be forced out. He would've had to be caught out, with no chance to argue against the true nature of his appetites.

"Shut up!" Walker had hissed. "We are here to discuss your silence on this matter!"

Walker had demanded Fane's silence in exchange for his own.

"You can play at being this 'Lord Galbreth' if you please, Peter White," he said the name with vicious relish. "But my silence will only last so long as your own silence. If so little as a whisper against me reaches my ears, I will call in the constabulary, and haul you before a naval board before you can spell the word 'deserter.' "

There had been nothing left to say after that. The only good to come out of the discourse was that each man clearly understood the other. That had been Fane's intent when he had asked Walker to join him outside. He had never expected Walker to be so anxious that the man had been forced at first to clasp his hands together in a vain attempt to hide their shaking. Then had come that peculiar moment, as clear as glass, when Walker's apprehension had fled, and his attack had begun.

What had Fane said? What had changed? Was the man simply a lunatic? He must be, to abuse his power as captain as he always had, to do what he did to young boys. . . .

And now, here was Walker, whispering more words in Marietta's ear, words even more dangerous than the poisonous lies Walker had surely told about Fane. But these words, to judge by Marietta's blushes, were more dangerous yet . . . because they were words of courtship.

"Lord Galbreth?" Miss Partridge's voice at last penetrated the roaring in Fane's head, and he thought she must have said his name several times.

"Sorry," he mumbled. "Warm in here. Not myself. Travel, you know," he excused himself, and everyone politely nodded even though he'd been on solid ground better than a week. "I think I will bid you all a good night," he said, moving through the circle of guests almost before he was done speaking.

He was stopped halfway to the exit from the foyer, however, by a too-familiar voice. "You will have to wish me happy," Mr. Walker said, stepping slowly from an adjoining room toward Fane, Walker's great-coat hanging over his arm, making it clear he was also preparing to leave. Fane glanced about, vaguely hoping someone else would step in and stop this worm, this vermin from speaking to him, but no one else was near except a footman.

"I wish you to hell," Fane said on a growl.

The eyes of the footman by the door grew a little wider, and he clearly strained forward to hear more. He was doomed to be disappointed, however, for Walker spoke in a low tone intended for Fane's ears alone.

"Are you not curious why you should wish me happy? No? I will tell you anyway. I have asked Miss Hampton to marry me."

Fane felt his hands curl into tight fists. "And her answer?"

"Well," Walker shrugged, and gave an amused little *moue* of a smile. "She has very properly said she wishes to think about it a while, but, in case you do not know it, Galbreth, she has no hope of any other offers. She is *de trop* in most polite society, the result of her own actions. She may be *tolerated* here, but surely even you have to admit there is scarcely a stream of beaux begging for her penniless hand. So you see, I expect she and I will be announcing the glad news as soon as may be."

Walker began to turn away, but then he twisted back, holding up his forefinger as if just having a thought. Fane tensed, knowing the gesture always bode ill.

"Lord Galbreth," he said the name on a sneer, "I do hope you will remember our conversation. Be a clever fellow and refuse any belated temptation to play the part of knight errant. Telling Miss Hampton anything will only ruin this chance for her. And as I say, I am all the chance for marriage that she has."

Walker moved away, his hands folded behind his back in military style, a light whistle trailing in his wake.

Fane turned blindly to the footman, and gruffly demanded his coat. The wait was long, too long. He wanted to leave at once, to be out of doors, to clear his head with the cool night breezes. . . .

He lifted his gaze, striding back to the entry that would allow him to see into the hall where the musicians were once again tuning their instruments. He walked almost against his own will . . . except that he had to look at Marietta, had to read her honest gaze for himself.

As soon as he came to the room's threshold, their gazes collided across the room, and he wondered if she had been looking for him as well. Could it be? But, perhaps not, for immediately she threw her gaze to the carpet beneath her feet, her face going very pale, as though in shock or loathing.

But the glance had lasted long enough for Fane to be sure of two things. It was true: Walker had asked her to marry him.

And she was considering telling the man "yes."

He could understand her logic completely: like himself, Marietta was not one to accept what she had not earned. She had avoided him all night, doing everything she could to avoid being with Fane. Since she was deliberately refusing to be at his side as his tutor, she would consider that she had broken their bargain, that she no longer deserved the right to remain in the dower house. Where, then, was she to live? Mr. Walker had made her an offer, a way for Marietta to keep a roof over her and her aunt's heads, a way that she dare not casually dismiss.

As soon as Fane had his great-coat and hat in hand, he went out the door, not bothering to don either. Once he was seated in his carriage rolling toward Westby Hall, feeling chilled despite the night's relative warmth, he sat back hard against the squabs.

His decision was made in a moment. There really was not anything to decide, after all.

He must speak to Marietta, must tell her who and what Walker was.

He could not let his own ambitions, his growing appreciation of the Kendall Town populace, his own need to find a home, keep him from saving Marietta from the role Walker meant her to play, to the degradation that would be hers if . . . *when* Walker was so worthless and stupid as to allow his dark, terrible secret to be discovered a second time. Fane had no doubt that the man's appetites had not changed any more than had his cruel streak, nor had the arrogance that would always lead to discovery.

Walker could not be allowed to ruin yet another life, another good, worthy soul. For Marietta was all that, despite anything else she might be. What good would a new life be to Fane, a new home, if Marietta was harmed to gain it? No, not Marietta—brave, strong, lovely Marietta.

"Marietta," he whispered her name, and closed his

eyes, but the ruse did nothing to block her face from his mind's eye. Honest, direct Marietta. He must be equally direct, he vowed. "You cannot accept him," he said to the panels of the coach, as though the saying would make it so.

But it would not. Only one thing might serve the trick: tomorrow Fane would tell Marietta everything she needed to know—and his secret, his future, be damned.

Fourteen

"That you, m'lord?" the investigator asked the next morning as he hooked a thumb at the painting hanging up behind Fane. Fane glanced over his shoulder at the painting, now illuminated by the slanting morning light coming in through the nearby window. He'd had the painting removed from his father's bedchamber and placed here, behind this desk at which his father used to sit. Fane sat here now, slowly grasping the ins and outs of how to manage his father's large estate . . . to say nothing of the notices he received from the London house, the houses his papa had apparently kept in Bath and Brighton, the thousand acres in Kent, and the shipping interests out of Cornwall.

"Yes, that is me," Fane told the investigator, Mr. Thornton, as he turned back to face him. "On my father's knee. I like having it in here with me."

The investigator nodded approvingly.

"I take it you have a report for me," Fane suggested.

"I found out about your cousin, sir. Private Malcolm Westby."

"As expected," Fane said on a nod. "What did you learn of him?"

"Word is he's a fair man. A wee bit of a stiff, according to some chaps in Chelsea Hospital, in London, what knows him, but good enough in a fight they say. One to make up his own mind, rather'n follow along they says. He's got money on his own, too. He din't join the army for the blunt it'd earn him, but for the glory or some such. His older brother died, so he's inherited his brother's estate. It ain't large, sir, but he could retire if'n he wanted to right enough. He's in the army for the fun o' it, it seems."

"The fun of it!" Fane echoed, thinking that his three weeks in the Royal Navy had been enough to prove his cousin either very brave or rather stupid.

"That is it then," he said aloud, slapping the flat of his hand against the table. "My cousin has no need of this estate or its money, and no apparent interest in staying about to manage his own, let alone another." Fane looked up at Thornton, who nodded in agreement.

"He don't seem likely to resign his commission, m'lord."

Now it was Fane's turn to nod again. "I will write to him, and invite him to visit," he said, frowning for a moment over the thought that Russia might well put an end to any hope of a meeting between him and his cousin—but he had no control over that. The only thing Fane had control over was this estate.

Because he now knew he *did* have control—the solicitors' letter had arrived this morning. It had read simply:

Direction: Fane Westby, Lord Galbreth, Westby Hall
Dear Sir:
    Please pardon the delay in this response to your in-

quiry. Our offices and its members have recently been beset by an unfortunate onslaught of the grippe. We have yet to host sufficient numbers of healthy officers to comply with your desire for a reading of your father's will, but until this formality may be attended to, I wish to inform you from personal knowledge that your father did indeed designate your person as his heir. Whereas this had previously been designated in absentia, *upon receipt of your recent letter, your father specifically requested a change to indicate your direction in America, and your improved status as his located heir. The document was duly signed and witnessed.*

Please be aware that in anticipation of his passing, your father established operating funds for your convenience, via the Kendall Town bank. Included is a letter of introduction, which will serve to initiate this account in your name.

It is my greatest wish that you will accept this breach from proper etiquette in the spirit in which it is intended, and I look forward to personally attending to the reading of your father's will as soon as may be.

> *Sincerely yours,*
> *Edmund Hopkins, Solicitor*
> *Brown, Harding, and Hopkins*
> *Staple Inn, High Holborn, London*

Unfortunately, the letter said nothing about the dower house, and whether or not Fane's papa had intended the ladies to have it.

"No matter," Fane said, sitting up straight.

"M'lord?" Thornton questioned with a puzzled look.

Fane dismissed his own words with a wave of his

hand, for Thornton did not need to know that Fane
had decided to gift the ladies with the dower house.
He did not need to know that Fane hoped the assurance that they were to have a roof over their heads
until they no longer wished it would be enough to
entice Miss Hampton, Marietta, to decline the marriage offer from Walker.

"As to that other matter, m'lord," Thornton said,
recapturing Fane's full attention. "I couldn't find out
much there, m'lord, but it's clear enough that this
Walker bloke were made to leave his office. He's getting no pension, I found out that much. Disgraced,
he were, I thinks—that being why the records is so
hard to get a look-see at, o' course. Something smelled
bad there, else'n why'd they lock up the records so
right and tight, eh? It's clear enough the navy don't
want no word of the captain's antics getting about, I
say."

"I daresay you are right," Fane said, reaching into
his desk to pull out a money packet. "That's an end
to your investigations then, Mr. Thornton. I appreci-
ate your efforts."

Thornton took the packet, slipping it in his coat
pocket with obvious satisfaction. He gripped the brim
of his hat in a salute. "Jest be sure to tell others o' my
good work, sir, should they need it."

"I will."

"Oh, and, sir?"

"Yes?" Fane asked, rising to come around the desk.

"I learned a little bit about that filly—er, about the
young miss, Miss Hampton by name, m'lord, if 'n
you'd care to hear it?"

Fane opened his mouth to decline the offer—whatever it was, it could not disprove the truth as he knew it of Marietta—but Thornton charged on. "She shot her betrothed. One source said what the man was kilt, but another said he had to have his foot cut off, to save him from the gangrene, m'lord. But I saw Mr. Sharr—that's his name—myself, not two months past, and he were walking well enough. I don't believe for a minute he's got a wooden leg, myself, but I do know no one dares to mention Miss Hampton's name to him. He knocked out the tooth of some young buck what was fool enough to ask if Mr. Sharr were still engaged to her."

"I . . . I see," Fane said, feeling for a moment unsteady. Not from the idea that Marietta might have shot someone—he'd faced her pistol himself when he'd first arrived—but at the information that Marietta had been betrothed.

"Walker!" he said suddenly, the word a curse, because Walker knew what had happened between Marietta and this fiancé of hers. The man was not above telling the tale to others, not if it kept other beaux at bay, left Marietta isolated and vulnerable to his pursuit of her. Walker, who was not above blackmailing Marietta into granting him the respectability he had lost and now craved to restore.

As soon as Mr. Thornton had mounted and rode away down the long drive, Fane threw on his hat, and neglected to pull on any gloves—a landlubber's tendency he was slow to adopt—and strode from his house. There was no time like the present to call upon Marietta and explain Walker's past . . . and to tender his own goodbyes, for Fane had no doubt that the minute Walker knew what Fane had done, Walker's revenge would be swift.

Marietta came to the door of her bedchamber, her hands unsteady on its frame, and peered toward the front door of the dower house.

Lord Galbreth stood outside, and Mr. Walker had frozen where he held the door open. The two men stared at one another, neither bothering to disguise their hatred of one another.

How dare Mr. Walker open her door—how would it look, with her aunt gone from the house? And to open it to find Lord Galbreth on the other side—! The shaking in Marietta's hands stilled, as if they could no longer reflect the confused emotions that rampaged through her.

"What is it?" Marietta asked, coming from her room.

Lord Galbreth did not answer her question, instead asking one of his own. "What are you doing here?" It was directed at Mr. Walker.

"That is not your concern. Miss Hampton is busy, so I suggest—"

Galbreth reached for Walker's shoulder, and before the man could react, had shoved him out of the doorway. Walker spun, sputtering in indignation. "Miss Hampton! I insist you order this cretin from your home," he demanded.

"It is not my home. This building belongs to Lord Galbreth," Marietta said, amazed by her own calmsounding voice. Why did these men hate each other so much? Even if Galbreth had chosen to believe a rumor, it did not explain the waves of animosity that rolled between the two. Mr. Walker had not told her something, something important, something that might make sense of the incomprehensible claims he had made against Lord Galbreth, the claims that made less and less sense to her with each garment she had folded to place in her valise.

"My lord," she turned to Galbreth. "May I assist you in some way?"

"Yes," he said, taking a seat uninvited.

Marietta sat opposite, feeling none of the warmth from the coals just burning themselves out on the grate of the fireplace. She folded her hands in her lap, hands that had just been packing to leave.

Walker strode forward angrily, throwing himself down on the cushion next to Marietta. "You should know, Galbreth, that Miss Hampton has agreed to be my wife."

"We are going to—I was just packing to . . ." she could not finish her statement, for the missing word seemed suddenly strange to her, even wicked.

"We are going to elope!" Mr. Walker supplied, his arm snaking about her waist. Marietta looked down at it, and thought of Mr. Sharr and how she had shot him in his foot, how all the changes in her life had come about beginning at that unfortunate moment.

"Elope!" Lord Galbreth repeated, and the word sounded even uglier when he said it.

But why shouldn't she elope? She had done everything else of which Society did not approve—why not this one last transgression? If she eloped, then she could be married the sooner, and away from this dower house. She would be safe, at long last, with no more worries. Well, perhaps one—Mr. Walker had not promised that Aunt Silvia could come to live with them, but neither had he refused. Perhaps she could persuade him that the favor could be his bridal gift to her.

It would be good to no longer be beholden to Lord Galbreth—so why did Marietta's eyes sting as if she might shed tears at any moment?

Lord Galbreth sat forward, looking wearied. She wanted to reach out a hand to him, to soothe his brow by pressing her lips to it . . . truth was, she wanted to press her lips to his mouth. That was why she was sad, of course: she loved Galbreth . . . Fane. She certainly did not love Mr. Walker. She had never even uttered Mr. Walker's Christian name . . . but he was the one she would marry, to free Fane of the burden of her company, her scandalous past, the rumors that would always follow her and taint any man who wanted to . . . *Silly girl,* she silently chided herself, *Fane does not want anything of the likes of you!*

"No," Galbreth said, quietly.

"Eh?" Walker said, his gaze narrowing.

"My lord?" Marietta inquired with a small, uncomprehending frown.

"No, you will not elope with this man."

"I will not?" Did she sound as stupid as she felt? Did Fane not realize it was only to his good for her to marry as soon as may be?

"You will not. And I will tell you why not. My name is Fane Westby, but I lived under another name in America, that of Peter White. It is under this name that Captain . . . Mr. Walker knows me," he confessed resolutely.

Mr. Walker howled in outrage, an animalistic sound that made the hairs stand up on the back of Marietta's neck. "Go no further, White! Not one word more, or I will see you in the field!"

"A duel?" Galbreth looked faintly amused. "Come now, Walker, even I know that a duel would be illegal."

"If you speak, it will be worth any exile I might have to suffer to see your blood spilled!" Mr. Walker hissed.

"Nonsense," Galbreth said. "You have gone out of your way to avoid exile from England. I doubt you will risk it for my sake. There are so many other ways to see a man dead, you know, rather than to fight a duel with him."

"You bastard—!"

Galbreth held up a hand. "Ah-ah! I would not start calling names, were I you. There are so many choice ones I might throw back at you."

He then ignored Mr. Walker, who leaped up to stand with white-knuckled hands gripping the back of an upholstered chair, as Galbreth turned to fit his attention on Marietta. He spilled out a sordid tale of trespass and indignities upon the high seas, a tale of a brutal, depraved captain named Walker.

Of a sudden, part way into the account, Mr. Walker turned without word, storming across the room, his head held high with outrage as he slammed himself out the door, leaving Marietta and Galbreth alone together.

Galbreth noted the exit, and turned back to Marietta. "I will be surprised if he has gone to fetch his seconds," he noted wryly before going on to finish the recital of Walker's offenses.

When it was all told, Marietta sat very still, more

undone by the fact that everything made sense than that it did not. She might have married that man, might have had to learn his true nature later, after she had made a vow to him. . . .

The mutual hatred between the two men now made perfect sense, as did Mr. Walker's unkind lies—for Marietta now knew they had been nothing more than lies, whispered to manipulate her in ways Walker was clever enough to know they would.

"I could not let you marry him," Galbreth said quietly as he sat forward, his elbows on his knees, his hands clasped before him.

Marietta still felt stunned, but there was a growing and overwhelming sense of relief as well. Relief? That her only means of changing the status of her life had just walked out? Oh yes, there was relief enough to learn what manner of man she had narrowly escaped pledging herself to, but so much more relief to learn that Galbreth was not the man who had been full of deceit, not the one deserving of having aspersions heaped on his good name. Whatever his name might be, Marietta thought, coughing to cover a small wrought-up laugh.

Galbreth hung his head for a moment, his brows coming together in a deep scowl. "I am only sorry that I did not tell you the truth about this man the minute I first set eyes on him again."

"Why did you not?" Marietta asked.

"Because he knew that other name, the one I had grown up being called."

Marietta stared at Fane. "But . . . why? Why was that a threat? Did you think your father would mind the other name? But, that cannot be it, for your father was gone before you ever met up again with Mr. Walker . . . ?"

Galbreth shook his head, looking sheepish. "Walker knew that I had deserted his ship, of course, or at least that is how he would have reported it to the Royal Navy, make no mistake. He has only to identify me to the authorities, and I shall be arrested as a deserter."

Marietta put a hand to her throat, and shook her head. "No!" she said at once. "No, that is not true."

Now it was Galbreth's turn to shrug. "I suppose if I leave at once for the coast, I might secure a return packet to America before the authorities are able to apprehend—"

"No!" she interrupted. "You do not need to sail anywhere! Did you not know, Lord Galbreth, that there is a way for a man to be free of impressment?"

"What?" he cried, his eyes widening.

"Sometimes men are pressed who, either by law or circumstance, are not allowed to be pressed! They have only to obtain protection—that is, a certificate of exemption—and they must be set free!"

"I—! It sounds too simple to be true," he protested, but there was a ring of hope in his tone.

"I *know* it is true! The impressment laws were fiercely debated in the House of Commons during the recent war with America, and they were all printed in the news sheets. I read them myself, and I argued against them with my brothers!"

"But," Galbreth sputtered, "but surely 'tis a matter of influence? I know no one of influence, no one who could obtain such an exemption for me. And my service was a year in the past. And although most of the lads were American born, I could not claim that justification for release, even if anyone were interested in listening—"

"My lord, it is a matter of money only! You have but to write to your magistrate and explain the circumstances—an illegal impressment of an American ship during the recent difficulties!—and supply something on the order of ten guineas to afford the hiring of a recruit to replace your lost service, and then you would be legally declared clear of any such charges!"

"My God!" Galbreth cried, both hands pressing to his head, and then slowly raking through his hair, his expression astonished. He looked up abruptly, understanding writ clear on his face. "That was it, then! I said something to Walker that let him understand I thought he had that power over me, that ability to see me hanged as a deserter! That was why he turned from a cowering dog into the aggressor!"

Marietta watched as the promise of reparation, of a burden lifted, filled Fane's eyes so that they glowed with hope.

He slid from his chair onto one knee before her, taking up her hand, staring back into her eyes. "The choice is mine now, you tell me! Once this business of the exemption is settled, that is. Then there will be nothing to make me leave England. I can be a free man!"

"Yes. It is true. Oh, I am so glad," Marietta said, and meant it. She left her hand in his, soaking up his joy, his happiness, knowing her own must come from some other place, some other future, away from his.

Even though Galbreth had never said those unkind words about her, even though it might seem she could go back to living in the man's dower house, Marietta knew she could not. Not and be so near to him, not now that she knew she loved him. She had borne so much, had found so many ways to keep going, but to be practically within arm's reach of the man she loved and yet never be able to touch him—that was at last more than Marietta could bear.

She wanted to ask Fane why he had come to keep her from marrying Mr. Walker, she wanted to think that the depth of emotion she felt for him might be returned in some small measure, but she dare not. A lifetime of disappointments had not prepared Marietta for the desolation she would feel if Fane gave a lukewarm answer about "duty to her gender" or some such noble but impersonal inanity.

How could she ever have imagined this man could be cruel? He was the very opposite—

The door slammed open, revealing Mr. Walker standing, his feet spread in raw aggression, a furious mask erasing any sign of human kindness from his features. He held a box under either arm, and he paced into the room, leaving the door open behind him as he slammed the boxes down on the nearest tabletop, throwing back their lids. One box held swords, the other pistols.

"Choose your weapon!" Mr. Walker said in a tone that was more growl than speech.

Fifteen

"It seems I was mistaken," Lord Galbreth said to Mr. Walker in a droll tone. "You *are* willing to risk exile for my sake."

"For the sake of seeing your miserable blood spilled," Mr. Walker said, several tiny droplets of spittle marking his lips and chin.

"He is mad," Marietta whispered, staring in horror.

Galbreth smiled at her, but there was wariness in that smile all the same. "I was right, however, about his not bringing seconds back with him, was I not, Marietta?" He did not give her the opportunity to answer, standing and walking over to survey the contents of the boxes. "Your private sets, I presume?" he said casually to Walker. "No doubt often used to help rid yourself of pesky, tattling cabin boys."

"Choose!" Walker howled.

"It is a difficult choice. And I am not sure I see the point of a duel any longer. That is, unless you propose to also dispose of Miss Hampton? After all, she has heard all I had to say. And she can testify against you regarding the duel." He shrugged. "Presuming I lose."

"Stop! You must stop this!" Marietta cried, rising to her feet. "I will swear to say nothing of Mr. Walker's past. All I ask in return, sir," she faced him, not hiding the loathing that filled her, "is that you swear to leave Kendall Town and never return."

"I, too, could be convinced not to speak." Lord Galbreth cast a quick glance toward Marietta, and she noticed he kept moving, putting his body between hers and Mr. Walker, shielding her. "For her sake, not for yours," he said to Walker.

The former captain curled his lips, a sick approximation of a smile. "Once you are dead, Galbreth, there is nothing to stop me from marrying her. She'll stay silent then, if she knows what's good for her."

Galbreth's face turned to stone, and he reached out to pick up a pistol. "Very well then," he said grimly.

Walker picked up the other pistol, and the leather bag beside it filled with powder and shot. "Outside." He flicked his head, indicating their removal from the house, his hands already opening the shot bag.

"No!" Marietta cried, running to Walker's side, stopping him from proceeding. "No, I will not allow this!"

"You have nothing to say to it. It is a matter of honor," Walker told her, shrugging off her hands where they clutched his arm.

"Honor? You would have to display some inkling of it first before we could call this a matter of honor," Galbreth taunted.

"Fane!" Marietta cried in despair, knowing his words had the power to drive the other man into a killing rage. "You must not do this! He is a trained military man. He knows how to shoot with precision."

" 'Fane'?" Fane echoed, his mouth curving ever so slightly, and a warm glow making his eyes turn to an even deeper blue. "How well that sounds, when you say it."

"Please do not do this," Marietta said through lips that felt half-numb.

"I am sorry," Galbreth replied, his smile fading.

"No! Swear! Swear to me that you will not speak of Mr. Walker's transgressions, if I ask it of you," Marietta said, moving to block Fane's way.

"Do not ask it of me. It is time this miscreant—"

"Swear it!" she cried, not able to keep the tears from springing to her eyes. She ignored them, blinking them out of her vision, so that two twin lines rolled down her cheeks.

"I swear it," Fane said softly, putting out his hand to run his thumb along her cheek, brushing at the tear track there.

She caught his hand under hers, then took a deep breath, released his hand with nearly a sob, and spun to face Mr. Walker. "I have his word! He will not speak!"

"His word is meaningless—" Walker began a retort.

"Not given to me, it is not. His word, given to me, he will keep," Marietta interrupted. "If what you want is respectability, sir, if what you want is our silence—we give it. I give it. I will marry you, and keep the secret of why you had to leave the navy. There, that satisfies your honor, sir. Are you man enough to take my offer?"

"Marietta—!" Fane said in a curiously soft reprimand.

She spun to face him. "I will not let him kill you!"

"Such little faith in my ability! I am not an entirely poor shot, you know," he argued, with that curious half-smile playing about his mouth. "Besides," he added, interrupting the obviously negative response Mr. Walker had meant to issue, "I cannot allow you to marry him."

"I will do as I want!" she declared, hotly and perversely arguing for the last thing she wanted on this earth—but it was worth it, worth the rest of her life if Fane were not shot and killed before her very eyes.

"Marry me instead," Fane said, and the three of them went still. "It solves the issue neatly. Walker cannot force you into a marriage if you are married to me instead. It would be his word versus the word of both of us. I am willing to wager that any crimes he might care to accuse us of would fall before the testimony we could give, the two of us, man and wife."

"But, what of your *honor!*" Walker snarled. "If you refuse to meet with me on the field of honor, marrying her makes no difference at all. You will be branded a coward."

"Perhaps so. It only matters if I care to measure myself by your standard of *honor,*" Fane said. He leaned to put the pistol down on the nearest table. "The problem is that I do *not* care. I already know you have nothing to tell the authorities about me that I am not free to tell them myself!"

Walker paled, and threw a malicious glance at Marietta.

"So, please, tell everyone you see that I refused to meet with you! Tell them that I have no honor—and I will tell them what *your* idea of honor has allowed you to do in the past."

Whatever color that had been left in Walker's face drained away, and his mouth worked soundlessly for a moment. But then an inhuman cry ripped from his throat, and he lunged at Fane, both hands lifted high to bring the unloaded pistol down on Fane's head.

Marietta dashed forward, meaning to somehow grab his hands, his arm, but instead the full brunt of the pistol's butt slammed into her right forearm, and she heard a sickening crunch and felt a poker-hot fan of pain clear up into her shoulder. She sank to the floor, too dizzy with pain to command her legs to hold her up.

Another cry filled the room, but it was not Marietta's; it was Fane's, an enraged roar as he surged toward Walker. His hands found and caught the off-balance Walker. Walker was dragged, unable to quite get his feet under him as he twisted and kicked, and there was a flurry of motion as the two men struggled for dominance.

Marietta whimpered, not from the pain in her cradled arm, but because she saw that Walker's hand reached out, almost touching the pistol Fane had set down on the table.

"Fane!" she warned weakly, but it was too late, because Walker already had his hand on the gun. He began to raise it, but with another cry, Fane twisted, throwing his weight against the smaller man's side, the two of them sprawling on the table. Another lunge and Fane had smashed Walker's hand back to the table top, and Walker screamed for the fingers that were undoubtedly broken as the pistol went skidding out of his grasp, clattering onto the floor. Fane pulled back, as if to lever his weight off Walker, but then he surged downward again, all his weight behind the curled fist he slammed into Walker's jaw. Fane pulled back his fist to strike again, but before he could, Walker slid bonelessly from the table to the floor, his head making a loud thump as it hit the floor.

Marietta stumbled to her feet, her legs so unsteady she almost fell to the floor again, but she forced her knees to lock. She surged toward the table, one step, two, and then stooped to gather up the pistol with the one hand that was capable of lifting it. She brought it up, gasping at the pain in her unsupported arm, and hefted the weapon near her ear, ready to come around the table and strike.

Fane stumbled upright, and looking at Marietta, shook his head. "He is unconscious." He took several jagged breaths, but then he grinned at her. "By gad, you are a brave one!"

The pain in her arm receded for a moment under the praise. "No more than you, to offer for me the way you did," she said, laughing a little. "A brilliant ploy, that."

When he did not laugh with her, she sobered and added, "I do not hold you to that offer, of course. You need not fear I am so foolish as all that."

"I have never once thought of you as foolish." He grinned. "I will admit that the words 'stubborn' and 'eccentric' have entered my mind, but never 'foolish,' Miss Hampton."

"Marietta," she said, because she had liked it so well when he had called her thus, because she would have too few more chances to hear her name from his lips.

"Marietta," he agreed. "And you must continue to call me Fane."

She looked away, unable to meet his gaze, but she nodded her agreement. What matter this informality, when she was so soon to go away anyway? Perhaps, if she wrote to Papa, he would allow her to return to London, if she promised to marry Mr. Sharr or anyone else Papa suggested. Perhaps her husband would be kind enough to give Aunt Silvia a home—or perhaps, yes, most likely, Fane would not mind allowing Silvia to remain here where her friends were. Fane had said he liked Aunt Silvia.

"You are in pain," Fane said, crossing to her.

Yes, Marietta thought, *but compared to my heart, my arm scarcely hurts at all.*

He made her sit on a sofa, and he gingerly examined her arm. "It is broken," he declared. "But just the one bone. It can be easily reset. The local surgeon seems a good man."

Marietta nodded. "Dr. Hammill. He pulled a tooth for Aunt Silvia." Was she babbling? Small wonder, with what they had been through . . . with Fane sitting so close to her, tending to her.

"Where is your aunt? I could certainly use her at the moment, if I am to ride out and fetch Dr. Hammill and—" Fane stopped in mid-sentence.

Marietta followed where he gazed, and gasped aloud.

Mr. Walker was gone, and one of the pistols with him.

Sixteen

Fane waited in the dower house doorway, bidding Marietta rest on the sofa. When she asked what he saw, he only shook his head. He had circled the house's interior several times, looking out windows, watching to see if Mr. Walker would return, but now he remained in the doorway, his attention fixed in one direction.

"Your aunt is coming in the gig," he said after a short while.

Marietta tried to sit up, the action jarring her arm enough to make her gasp. "Is she in any danger? From Walker?"

Fane shook his head. "Not unless I am much mistaken."

He did not explain that cryptic remark, and turned to lift a hand in greeting to Silvia. When she pulled the horse to, he walked out and offered to see to the rig and the horse for her.

Aunt Silvia accepted, her voice a familiar comfort as it carried in to Marietta, but when she entered, Marietta could clearly see her aunt was distraught.

"What is it?" Marietta asked without greeting, struggling again to sit up.

"Marietta!" her aunt cried upon spying the rough sling that supported her niece's arm. "You are hurt!"

"Yes. And I will explain, but first tell me why you are so overset."

"Why, Marietta! It is the most dreadful thing! I found his body, you see, coming home not this hour past from Mrs. Mulliton's. Mr. Walker's body! Just at the top of the rise. His head was . . . Suffice it to say he had suffered a terrible wound to his head, by gunshot! You must have heard the discharge? He is dead, Marietta." Her aunt's voice dropped into a low tone. "They say it is evident he killed himself."

Marietta nodded. She had indeed heard the gunshot, and standing guard with the other pistol belonging to Mr. Walker, Fane had heard it, too. It seemed clear that he must also have seen the body fall to the earth, for when she had asked him what the shot signified, Fane had only answered, "It is over."

Marietta did not feel the satisfaction she thought she might at this confirmation of Mr. Walker's death, but a kind of gratitude that at long last he had done something that bordered on noble. Or perhaps it was not so noble, but the final act of cowardice, a confirmation of how he had lived his whole life.

"I had to get some men to see to the body, and I had to make a report to the constable, else I would have been home ages ago!" Aunt Silvia went on. "But, my dear, whatever happened to *you*? How did you get injured? Has anyone gone for the surgeon?"

"Hetty came by not ten minutes ago, and Fane—"

"Fane?" Silvia echoed, looking astonished.

"Lord Galbreth," Marietta amended. "He sent

Hetty to fetch the surgeon. If Dr. Hammill is not otherwise engaged, he should be here any moment."

Silvia examined Marietta's arm, and declared it a clean break. "You will be back to your weaving in no time!"

Marietta explained how it had come to be injured. "It is just as well Mr. Walker has passed on," Aunt Silvia said darkly.

"Aunt Silvia!" Marietta pretended to scold, and then gladly accepted her aunt's offer of tea.

By the time Silvia had brought the tray of tea things next to the sofa, Fane returned from seeing to the horse. He quietly asked Silvia for the details of her unfortunate discovery. When that had been gone through again, Silvia rose. "I must see to readying my chamber for Marietta. No arguing, my girl! I am going to put you in my softer bed for at least the next week, and I will take your room."

Silvia bustled off to see to arranging the room as befitted an invalid, muttering something about the lack of timely courtesy displayed by surgeons these days.

Marietta smiled fleetingly at Fane. "Thank you, sir, for all you have done. But I would not keep you waiting here a moment longer."

"I want to wait," he said.

"You are so good, but I do not wish to tax your kindness. Aunt Silvia is here, and she will see to me until Dr. Hammill can arrive."

Fane made no move to stand and leave. "I wanted you to know the solicitors wrote to me. They have confirmed that I am to be my father's heir."

"That is as it should be," Marietta said softly.

"The letter from the solicitors said nothing about this house, what should be done with it."

"Ah. I see." She took a deep breath. "My lord, I have decided to—"

" 'Fane,' " he interrupted. "It is too late in the day for us to revert to 'my lord' this and 'Miss Hampton' that. You probably saved my skull from being crushed today, Marietta. That makes you my life-long friend, in case you did not know it."

"Friend," she repeated, then blushed at how silly she must sound. She had this much, then, at least: Fane had claimed her as a friend.

"I am giving this house to Miss Silvia," he said. He held up a hand as a signal that Marietta must refrain from replying. "My father told me before he passed away that no part of this property is entailed, so I am free to gift the house to someone if I so choose. And I do so choose. Miss Silvia is to have this house until she no longer wishes it."

"What if your wife objects to Silvia's presence?" Marietta asked.

"My wife? That would have to be you, would it not, or did you never accept my offer?" he teased.

Marietta just shook her head, not trusting her voice to keep from quavering.

"Your aunt will be more than happy to continue on as you both have, I daresay, sharing her home with you. So you see, Marietta, there is no longer any reason at all that you need to marry, except unless you should wish to," Fane said, his expression kind and sympathetic, so that she could scarcely bear to look at him.

He cleared his throat. "There is one other unfinished matter."

"Yes, the matter of my tutorship. I freely admit that I have not held up my end of the bargain—"

He shook his head. "There is no longer any bargain."

"Oh. Well, yes, I suppose that since you are going to give the house to my aunt, then . . ." She paused, utterly baffled as to what he could mean if he felt their bargain was already dissolved.

"You never accepted or rejected my offer of marriage," Fane explained, alternating glances between one of his fingernails and her face. Why, he almost appeared . . . shy.

"I wish you would not tease," Marietta said, and meant every word.

"I am not teasing."

"Then you are either deaf or mad. I already said I would not hold you to your offer. It was not even a real offer, anyway, so there was nothing to hold you to, to begin with."

"Nothing but my affections."

Marietta gasped. "Oh, now you go too far!" she said hotly, because if she spoke sternly she might not cry. "I am well aware I would never suit for a man like you."

"A man like me?" He seemed amused.

"Of course a man like you!" she cried with an agitated movement of her good hand. "You are wealthy, and landed, and well received by everyone in Kendall Town. They cannot cease talking about your goodness, about the pleasure of listening to your unusual accent, to the way you wear—" She cut herself off abruptly.

"To the way I wear what?"

She narrowed her eyes at him. "It is very poor form to torment an invalid," she informed him stiffly.

"To the way I wear what?" he repeated, and now she was sure he was laughing at her. Very well, she could dish the abuse right back at him.

"To the way you wear your . . . your unmentionables, if you must know! I overheard Miss Prentice say that she had never seen a pair of buckskins put to better use!"

Instead of flushing with embarrassment, Fane had the poor manners to roar with laughter. "And what about you?" he asked when he could, wiping at his eyes. "Do you agree with Miss Prentice?"

"You miserably vain creature!" she scolded.

"That is not an answer. In fact, you seem to have a great deal of difficulty answering any of my questions today. Let us return to the original one. Will you have me or not, Marietta?"

"Of course I will not! I would ruin any repute you have developed since your arrival. I am wholly unacceptable in the highest-flying circles, circles to which you could easily aspire."

"Wholly unacceptable? Why? Just because you shot someone named Mr. Sharr?"

Marietta sat up straight, little caring that she jarred her arm. "Walker must have told you that!" she declared.

"So it is true? I assume he was some manner of blackguard." He still smiled at her, the oaf.

"He was indeed. He was too stupid to understand that I would not marry him, and my father too stubborn to believe me when I refused."

"So, if I do not accept a refusal from you, are you

then going to shoot me? Where, exactly?" Fane winced, playacting, at least until Marietta flew from the sofa. Then he cowered even as he laughed aloud again. "You haven't a knife on you, have you?"

No, but the basket of threads she up-ended awkwardly with one hand over his head served her almost as well. Although all it did was make him laugh harder.

"No, no, I am perfectly, seriously curious," he said, when he could talk again.

Marietta stalked back to the sofa, pretending to fume but on the verge of laughter herself. After all, the subject of marriage between them was too silly for words.

"Where did you shoot this Mr. Sharr?"

"In the toe."

"In the toe?" He chortled.

"And I would do it again, in a moment, despite everything it led to."

He grinned at her. "I have no doubt." He sighed, and his expression sobered. He clapped his hands and rubbed them together, as if they were cold, although it was warm in the room. "So, you will not have me, eh? It is truly a pity. I need a wife, a family, a reason to be here in England, to build a life here."

"Well, I would not be that reason," she said. "Sooner or later the reason why my family banished me would become common knowledge, unavoidable. Here it has not mattered so much, but you will want to travel, to see London. There my history is a terrible scandal, believe me. I could not bring that kind of disgrace on you." She gave a small, tentative smile. "I have this history, as you have seen, of assaulting men. Besides," she said, putting up her chin, "I like my weaving. I would not want to give that up." She shrugged. "The marketing of it—now, that I would gladly forego, but the weaving itself—! Well, any husband of mine would have to know the loom goes with me, that I do not care tuppence that weaving is a task considered for the common laborer. In fact, I *am* a common laborer—"

"I have no objection to a loom in the house," he interrupted her to say.

"Enough," she said, her voice gone shaky. "Enough of this game," she insisted, not able to return his gaze.

His weight pressed down the cushion next to hers, and the tingling she had felt when he had kissed her hand now traveled all through her body, even though he did not touch her.

"It is not a game," he said, and then he did touch her, pulling her onto his lap as she gave a squeak of surprise. He was careful of her broken arm, but his hands at her waist kept her in place.

"You should have met my mama, Marietta," he said, looking up into her face. "I do not know if you would have liked her, but you would have understood her. She was strong, like you. Perhaps too strong. She made sudden decisions, and once made, they were seldom reversed. You might have had a softening influence on her—I do not know. But I do know that you are clever like her, and like her defiant of rules that make no sense, and willing to risk everything on the chance you might do better, might make a happy life for yourself."

Marietta stared down into his upturned face, scarcely daring to breathe.

"Perhaps I am a fool to admire you so. Heaven

knows that a bold woman is not a simple woman to live with. Perhaps I did not learn one thing from living all those years with a headstrong woman. Tell me one thing, and perhaps then I will understand . . . how could you promise to marry Walker, to let him go on living his depraved life any way he wished?"

His gaze was filled with something bordering on pain.

"I never said that. I promised to marry him, yes, and that I would never say a word about what had caused him to leave the navy. But I never said I would tolerate any more of the same kind of behavior."

Fane blinked, and then he pressed his forehead against her uninjured arm, and laughed a little.

"If I'd married him, and then had the smallest reason to think he might have designs to harm another lad . . . ! Well, I suppose I would have shot one of his toes off," she said firmly.

Fane moaned, and she thought she had disappointed whatever expectation he had formed—but the moan was only the beginning of a laugh, a deep, rich laugh in which she could not help but join.

"God save me, woman! If we married I would not dare have any firearms in the house!"

"Good thing you are not marrying me, I suppose," Marietta said as lightly as she could.

"I have another reason why I should be married to you," he said, and something in his voice caused them both to cease smiling, to sit very still.

"What is that?" she asked in the barest whisper.

"Because I have fallen in love with you."

"Ah," she said, not breathing.

"Marietta?"

"Yes?" It was more a squeak than a word.

"Is that reason enough for you to accept my offer of marriage?"

She hesitated, her thoughts passing over every word of this peculiar conversation, every nuance of his expressions. She remembered his enraged cry when Mr. Walker had struck her with the pistol. She remembered the horrified look he had given her when Walker had said they were planning to elope. Now he sat here, telling her he had fallen in love with her . . . and there was nothing to do but remember what manner of man this Fane Westby was.

"Of course that is reason enough," she said, and felt the corners of her mouth curve up as though to match the dawning smile on his face.

He kissed her then, pulling her head down so that her mouth could meet his for a long, lingering caress that left her little room to doubt him anymore.

"You had me a little worried there," he told her many long minutes later. "I scarce thought you were going to answer, let alone say yes."

"Even if I did not love you in return," she said, "I might have had to marry you anyway."

"Oh? And why is that?"

Marietta pointed to the window beside the door, from where the surgeon's startled face reared back. "I am afraid I have been compromised."

Aunt Silvia floated into the room, hurrying toward the door. "It is about time you settled things between you, you lovebirds. I have had to keep the doctor waiting for fully five minutes!"

The surgeon, when the door was opened to him

and he had entered, never did learn why the three occupants of the room were fully lost to laughter.

Fane sat before the fire in the sitting room between his bedchamber and the one he spent more time in, the one he had—these three months since the wedding—shared with his wife. They had waited for Marietta's twenty-first birthday to marry, after which she had been free to enter into wedlock without the consent of her parents.

He had the *London Times*—freshly delivered, which meant it was only two days out of date—open before him, resting unread on his knees. Instead he looked to his wife, Marietta, who was explaining some detail or other about a party they were invited to next week. They had postponed a bridal journey, Westby Hall somehow seeming the place to be in these first weeks of their marriage.

Marietta went on, saying how happy Hetty Dewlap was to have been made a chambermaid in their home, and that Dr. Hammill had said he thought he could do something in the nature of a brace and an elevated shoe to help the girl's gait. Marietta did not mention that this offer was helped along tremendously by her own offer to pay for the newfangled device.

She moved on to the matter of which of the new invitations they had received today would they accept, and Fane nodded or shook his head according to the names she mentioned. He listened, but truly he was busier watching her as she twisted and transformed a handful of dyed fleece into thread that wound about the spindle of the spinning wheel set before her chair.

She had a real talent at the craft—it was a pleasure to watch her turn a woolly mess into a skein of soft thread, ready for another transformation on her loom. She had missed performing the task while her arm healed, but the subsequent three months had seen a complete return of the arm's function.

"I received a letter from Papa today," Marietta said casually, but Fane knew the letter's arrival was anything but casual.

"Ought I to burn it?" he asked without judgment.

She shook her head. "Papa says he wishes to call upon us, if we will tell him when would be convenient."

Fane smiled. He did not need to tell Marietta that she had been right, that she must not go to her father, but rather her father must come to her if he desired a reconciliation. She had complied with her parents' every demand—a husband, with a title no less, and of sufficient income to make Mr. Sharr's thirty thousand pounds a year seem trivial—and yet Marietta had known she could not go to her father, would not pay the ransom he had put upon his affections.

Her mother had come to call first, upon the heels of reading the astonishing announcement of her daughter's marriage in the paper. She had come again two days later, this time with Marietta's brothers in tow, much to Marietta's surprise. The reunion had been somewhat awkward, but by the time her mother and brothers had left to make the hour's drive to London, pleasure had made Marietta's dark eyes shine like onyx.

One reunion, however, had remained unmade, one Marietta dare not initiate herself.

But now it had come to be, and under the terms Marietta had dictated. It did not matter if it were Fane's income, Marietta's respectability restored, or some other requirement that had been fulfilled—Marietta's papa had written to request that he might call upon her.

"Anytime that is convenient for you will serve me as well," Fane said.

"I will let you know what day," Marietta responded, a slight smile on her mouth.

Stubborn vixen, Fane dubbed his wife fondly and silently, the words far more for his father-in-law's sake than his own. Marietta was stubborn, yes, and outspoken, and determined—she possessed all the traits that earned women the various unkind titles such as the one he had just thought. But for all that these traits made life with her challenging, they also made it exciting, and interesting, and rewarding. Life would never be dull with Marietta in his home.

Perhaps that was the side of Mama that Fane's papa had missed, had literally let slip away. Perhaps Papa had forgot that while it is dangerous to play with fire, that flame also has the ability to warm you, to give light to your world, and that to stare into its flames is to believe in dreams and hopes.

Fane watched Marietta at her work a while longer, but then he moved the newspaper aside, and shuffled forward from his chair to his footstool, which brought his knee into contact with his wife's. She looked up at him, slowly shifting her concentration from the thread she worked to him. She smiled softly, an invitation.

"Look at us," Fane said, reaching under her dressing gown to find the curves beneath, as he drew her from her chair onto his lap. "Who would ever guess from the way I make free with your body that only a few months ago we were meeting for the very first time?"

"You with the dust of travel all about you," Marietta said, reaching to swirl a lock of his hair around her finger.

"You with a pistol readied to shoot me," Fane rejoined.

She buried her head against his neck and laughed, perhaps as much from his comment as from the fact he pressed noisy, wet kisses up her arm.

"I am glad I did not shoot you," Marietta said. "I have noticed men do not seem to want to marry me afterwards."

Fane chortled, rubbing his day's-growth of beard against her neck and making her squeal.

"Do you know, I have never got Mr. Sharr's direction from you," he commented, his lips now pressed against her throat.

"His direction?" Marietta questioned, and then she sighed as Fane began to nibble ever so gently just below her earlobe.

"Certainly," he mumbled, "I must call upon the man. But first, before I do, you will have to explain to me exactly which delicious, lovely, forbidden parts of you he dared to even attempt to touch."

"Why?" she murmured, her eyes closed with pleasure.

"So I may shoot him in a different digit for every offense he dared to offer you."

Marietta laughed throatily.

"You are a bloodthirsty wench, are you not?" Fane

teased, just before he moved his mouth to kiss first her top lip, then the other, then both at once.

After a while he stood, Marietta in his arms, and he carried her toward the bedchamber they shared every night. "I have something serious to propose," he said, even though part of him feared losing the soft, sensuous mood between them.

"What is it?"

"Sometime soon after your father calls upon us, I want to go to London. Both of us."

She did not stiffen in his arms, but she said rather sadly, "We will be rejected. You, the 'American,' and me the hoyden."

"Let us try. If then we are rejected, we will know," he suggested gently, not stooping to the trick of kissing her and trying to persuade her that way.

She sighed, but the sadness was gone from her voice. "All right then. Let us be brave."

"You know it does not matter anyway, do you not?" he asked, laying her on the bed, and joining her, lying half atop her. He tickled her nose with a lock of her own hair. "We do not need London. Or Philadelphia. Not even Westby Hall."

"I know," she said, wrapping her arms around his neck, and she did not have to say what they both already knew: that it was not a village, nor a city, not a people, nor a flawless reputation that could make them happy together. The vagaries of life would ebb and flow, but so long as they clung to one another, they would both be home.

Author's Note:

Kendall Town is a village of the author's invention, meant to approximate the many outlying and undeveloped areas that slowly grew within a one- or two-hour carriage drive of London in the early part of the nineteenth-century.

I enjoy hearing from readers!
You may write to me at:
Teresa DesJardien
P.O. Box 33323
Seattle, WA 98133

Please enclose a self-addressed, stamped envelope for a reply.

WATCH FOR THESE REGENCY ROMANCES